Story Telling Five

I0538162

December
2017

STORY TELLING

FIVE

STORY TELLING SERIES IS PUBLISHED
QUARTERLY

A compilation of short stories, yarns, rhymes and blogs.

SOME ARE LONG AND SOME ARE TRUE

THERE ARE ONES THAT ARE SHORT
AND OTHERS ARE BLUE

ALL ARE THOUGHT PROVOKING
WITH FUNNY ONES WORTH A GIGGLE OR TWO

STORY TELLING FIVE

MAGAZINE PUBLISHED QUARTERLY

ISBN 978 0 9956917 6 6

Published by

Percychatteybooks Publisher

© Percy W Chattey 2017

The Story Telling Series is looking for short stories, anecdotes for inclusion in our next issue, please send to percybooks@outlook.com all entries will be acknowledged.

Story Telling Five

As always for my lovely wife Jean, friend and soul mate, who has helped with the editing and all rewrites, also listening to all my ramblings whilst putting these articles together.

My appreciation to the following
Derek Cook for previous cover
Christopher Wyatt
Richard Seal
Lily-Ella Mainstone
Trudie Le Beau
Pete Broadbent
Richard Littlejohn
Leapy Lee
All my friends on Social Media who send me their gems.

Percy says to all our readers:
Happy Christmas and may the hinges of our friendship never grow rusty ...

My name is Meg and I will be your host throughout this product. But First let me explain the following as it is very important:

The contents and the opinion shown or written here are not necessarily the views of 'Story Telling' or its publisher and are published as articles of interest and amusement only and no offence of any kind religious, race or political is intended to any person or group of people.

**

As we enter the season of goodwill it is appropriate to start with a Christmas theme, our thanks to Chris Wyatt for this charming start to Story telling five.

Christmas Night

'Twas the night *after* Christmas,
And all through the house,
Not a creature was stirring
Not even a mouse.

For of Turkey and Ham, plum pudding and
such
Everyone there had eaten too much
Now in a somnambulant stupor they lay
Stretched out by the fire for the whole
of the day.

Just once in a while a voice could be
heard
"Will someone please bring me a slice of
the bird
And a small slice of ham, a potato or two
I'm not really hungry so that ought to do"

The floor was all littered with paper and
string

That had covered the gifts that
Christmas time brings
Garments and games, books, a plant in a
pot,
Things that were wanted and some that
were not!

Still the spirit of Christmas was patently
there,
The loving and giving, the choosing with
care
And the hope was expressed that
throughout the New Year,
All would be Happy and Healthy and full
of good cheer.

Copyright: Christopher Wyatt

**

We will, for the moment carry
on the Christmas theme, with a
nice piece from one of our
regular writers Richard Seal

Christmas Cake

Mark's childhood Christmases were cherished; chocolates, half-melted, always plucked from the fake tree with pure glee. Santa would sit sated after sherry and mince pies, happy watching Morecambe and Wise. Now the day only feels special while watching his young nieces and nephews at play.

Somehow all the adult festive fun seems anodyne, with virtual gifts bought online; For Mark, nothing seems quite the same, even the nostalgia feels lame. The Christmas period always seems to bring indolent indulgence, heavy drinking, excessive eating towards inevitable indigestion.

This year it is Mark's turn to host the dreaded pre-dinner party games where perils pervade, prevail ... A tipsy family friend leads charades, games involving matchboxes on noses, and any opportunity for balloons to be pressed, then passed, with paper hats askew. Mark's sister Anne skulk sidles around the room, avoiding awful Aunts and Uncle Harbinger of doom. However, Anne is foiled, her day spoiled by a second cousin with lusty kisses to bestow beneath the mistletoe.

After surviving the late afternoon turkey feast, there is no ignoring his mum's persistent imploring to delve into the box of sticky-sweet dates. However, the day's saving grace is the frisson of mum's annual Christmas cake, the thrill of the rich fruit with white icing and thick marzipan, which, for Mark, has always trumped all the toys. The crowning glory is a hefty hunk of her special heavy stuff - one piece is more than enough.

Copyright Richard Seal 2017

**

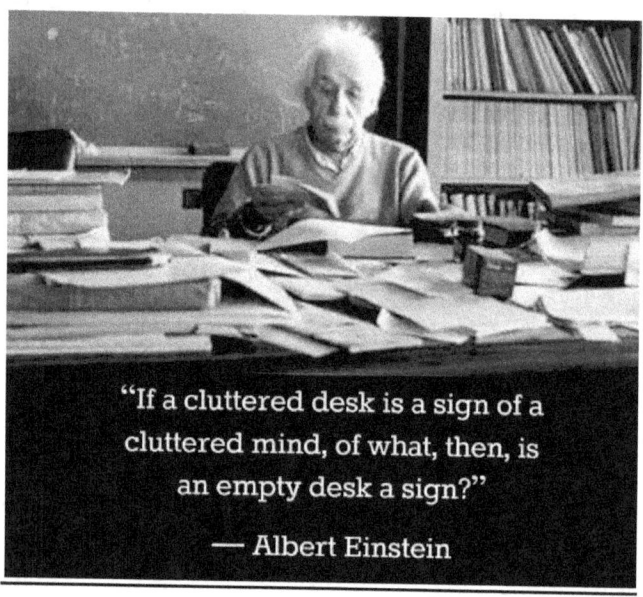

"If a cluttered desk is a sign of a cluttered mind, of what, then, is an empty desk a sign?"

— Albert Einstein

An old Woman was asked,
"At your ripe age, what would you prefer
to get : Parkinson's or Alzheimer's?"
The wise one answered, "Definitely
Parkinsons - Better to spill half my wine than
to forget where I keep the bottle."

Silence not so Golden

Earl and Bubba are quietly sitting in a boat fishing, chewing tobacco and drinking beer when suddenly
Bubba says, "Think I'm gonna divorce the wife - she ain't spoke to me in over 2 months."
Earl spits overboard, takes a long, slow sip of beer and says, "Better think it over....women like that are hard to find."

**

At a movie theatre, which 'arm rest' is yours?

In the word scent, is "S" silent or "C"?

If people evolve from monkeys, why are monkeys still around?

Why is there a 'D' in fridge, but not in refrigerator?

Who knew what time it was when the first clock was made?

If pro and con are opposites, wouldn't the opposite of progress be congress?

Bearing in mind Health and Safety it would be best to take the following advice throughout the Festive Season. By Anon:

All persons planning to dash through the snow in a one horse open sleigh, going over the fields and laughing all the way are advised that a Risk Assessment will be required addressing the safety of an open sleigh for members of the public. This assessment must also consider whether it is appropriate to use only one horse for such a venture, particularly where there are multiple passengers. Please note that permission must also be obtained in writing from landowners before their fields may be entered.

To avoid offending those not participating in celebrations, we would request that laughter is moderate only and not loud enough to be considered a noise nuisance. Benches, stools and orthopedic chairs are now available for collection by any shepherds planning or required to watch their flocks at night.

While provision has also been made for remote monitoring of flocks by CCTV cameras from a centrally heated shepherd observation hut, all users of this facility are reminded that an emergency response plan must be submitted to account for known risks to the flocks'

The angel of the Lord is additionally reminded that, prior to shining his/her glory all around, s/he must confirm that all shepherds are wearing appropriate Personal Protective Equipment to account for the harmful effects of UVA, UVB and the overwhelming effects of Glory.

Following last year's well publicised case, everyone is advised that Equal Opportunities legislation prohibits any comment with regard to the redness of any part of Mr R Reindeer. Further to this, exclusion of Mr R Reindeer from reindeer games will be considered discriminatory and discirplinary action will be taken against those found guilty of this offence.

While it is acknowledged that gift bearing is a common practice in various parts of the world, particularly the Orient, everyone is reminded that the bearing of gifts is subject to Hospitality Guidelines and all gifts must be registered. This applies regardless of the individual, even royal personages. It is particularly noted that direct gifts of currency or gold are specifically precluded, while caution is advised regarding other common gifts such as aromatic resins that may evoke allergic reactions.

Finally, in the recent instance of the infant found tucked up in a manger without any crib for a bed, Social Services have been advised and will be arriving shortly.

**

Wonder why the word funeral starts with FUN?

Confidence...

A fighter pilot walks into a pub and sits down next to a very attractive woman.

He gives her a quick glance then casually looks at his new Apple watch for a moment.

The woman notices this and asks, "Is your date running late?"

No, he replies, just got this state-of-the-art Apple watch, and I was testing it.

The intrigued woman says, A state-of-the-art watch? What's so special about it?

The pilot says, It uses alpha waves to communicate with me telepathically.

The lady says, What's it telling you now?

"Well, it says you are not wearing panties.

The woman giggles and replies, Well it must be faulty because I am!

The fighter pilot smiles, taps his watch and says, Damn thing's an hour fast!

And that, my friends......is **Confidence!**

**

If money doesn't grow on trees, how come Banks have Branches?

Ku Klux Klan?

An Alabama pastor said to his congregation, "Someone in this congregation has spread a rumour that I belong to the Ku Klux Klan. This is a horrible lie and one which a Christian community cannot tolerate. I am embarrassed and do not intend to accept this. Now, I want the party who said this to stand and ask forgiveness from God and this Christian family."

No one moved. The preacher continued, "Do you have the nerve to face me and admit this is a falsehood? Remember, you will be forgiven and in your heart you will feel glory. Now stand and confess your transgression." Again, all was quiet

Then, slowly, a drop-dead gorgeous blonde with a body that would stop a runaway train rose from the third pew. Her head was bowed and her voice quivered as she spoke, "Reverend there has been a terrible misunderstanding I never said you were a member of the Ku Klux Klan. I Simply told a couple of my friends that you were a wizard under the Sheets."

The preacher fell to his knees, his wife fainted, and the congregation Roared.

The Best Christmas Ever

By Trudie Le Beau

Brian and Sue Ballard were beyond ecstatic when they were contacted by the adoption authorities who were pleased to tell them that they had a two month old baby boy in need of a home. They were not in the first flush of youth and after many years of heartache they had resigned themselves to never having a child, so understandably they lavished all their love and affection on the little boy that they named Jamie, Roy. Unfortunately the old maxim of 'spare the rod and spoil the child' still holds true and by the age of seven Jamie had become – I hate to say it of a child – but he had become quite a horrid little boy.

It was the day before Christmas Eve and this year it was their turn to have Sue´s parents and her younger brother Tom and his family for the big day so she and Jamie had driven the three miles from their home into town to visit Dobson's toy shop.   "Now, I just need to get tree presents for Jack, Peter and Susie and then I want to pop into the grocers for a few last minute bits and then get home as quickly as we can, I´ve got such a lot to do."

Jamie was sulking; he wanted to play with some of the toys on display but mum wasn´t taking any notice today and his mood darkened. Then he saw the gleaming red engine pulling two red and cream carriages gliding past miniature stations, under bridges and through green countryside dotted with miniature sheep. He was mesmerised, "I want that."

"Well you will have to wait to see what Father Christmas brings you won´t you. Come on Jamie we don´t have time to dawdle today, what do you think about this little bracelet for Susie?"

He really wanted that train so he decided to do what he always did in order to get his own way; he threw himself to the floor and started screaming. He knew everyone was watching which encouraged him to scream so hard that in the end he could hardly breath and he had a coughing fit, but annoyingly this once it didn't work and mum actually grabbed him by the hand and pulled him out of the shop.

With Jamie protesting every step of the way they made their way back to the car park and, without saying a word, mum pushed him into the car and slammed the door. She didn't speak until they were back indoors. She marched him into the front room and turned on the television. "My afternoon has been ruined thanks to you and I haven't got half the things I wanted so you can just stay there while I run down to the corner shop without you." Jamie had never seen his mum like this, she looked really angry and her face was all red. "You just sit on that settee until I get back," and she actually shouted, "Or else!"

He heard the back door slam and unable to contain his anger he jumped up and kicked the paper covered pot holding the Christmas tree making it shake so that some of the glass balls fell off. "I suppose you think that was clever!"

Jamie stopped mid kick. He looked around but there was no-one in the room so he scowled and kicked the pot again. "You really are a horrid little boy aren't you? I'm going to tell Father Christmas not to leave you anything at all – you really don't deserve it."

The voice sounded cross and now he was a little scared and as there was no-one in the room he peeped behind the *curtains to see who was there – no-one!   "I'm up here, on top of the tree, and you nearly made my tiara fall off.   Look up boy, look at me when I'm talking to you."*

Jamie looked up but all he could see was the fairy on top of the tree and, he rubbed his eyes and looked again, she was moving her arms and pointing at him.   "I meant what I said young man. Unless you change your ways rapidly there will be no presents for you and that is an end to it."

"But, but…"

"But what - what should you do? I'll tell you what you should do. You should stop being such a horrid boy and think about others.   Your poor mother was thinking of others when she wanted to shop but you, you weren't thinking about anyone but yourself – shame on you."   The fairy leant forward "If from now on you behave yourself and try being kind and helpful for once I may, and I only say may, not tell on you, but I'll be watching so it's up to you – nice boy – or horrid."

Just then the door slammed and mum came into the room. "Oh for goodness sake what are all those decorations doing on the floor?"

"Oh I'm sorry mum I tripped and they fell off, don't worry I'll put them all back and can I help you with putting the shopping away and whip the cream for the trifle?"

Mum sat down.   This was not the reaction she had expected.   She watched Jamie leave the room carrying her basket and heard cupboard doors opening and closing. Who was this boy?

The next day mum was busy in the kitchen preparing and baking ready for tomorrow and with Jamie's help all the last minute jobs were done well before dad got home. After supper he had a bath and went to bed un-protesting leaving his parents waiting for the back lash that never came.   On Christmas morning they were all up with the lark. Dad poured out the tea and carried the tray into the front room, "Come on my dears, let´s undo our stockings and see what Father Christmas has left under the tree and you can undo one present Jamie then we'll wait for your cousins before we open the rest."

Jamie usually kicked off at this point as he hated waiting for the others but surprisingly he hung back.   He crossed his fingers, "Please, please, I´ve been good."

Dad exclaimed "My word, just look at this lot!"

Jamie peeped around the door and was overjoyed, she hadn't told on him!   He knelt before the huge pile of presents and could not resist feeling one of them.   It was hard and long and he just knew it was a train.   Dad helped him to pick it out of the pile and, heart thumping he slid his fingers under the paper fold and pulled it back revealing a shiny red engine.   "Oh thank you Santa, thank you, thank you, thank you."   He looked up at the fairy who looked so beautiful atop the twinkling tree lights and he smiled as she gave a small secret wave and winked.

Nan and Grandad, Tom, Sheila, Jack, Peter and little Susie arrived with arms full of presents and to the gorgeous aroma of roasting turkey.   They loved Sue and Brian but in truth had not been looking forward to spending the day with Jamie, but they were most pleasantly surprised to find that their misgivings had been unfounded and Jamie was as good as could be.   The huge meal had been delicious, the games had been such fun and Jamie had been so sweet, happily sharing his toys and joining in the laughter and games, and to make the day perfect it began to snow.

Story Telling Five

As the evening progressed the snow fell heavily and everyone ended up in the garden throwing snowballs in the dark and having such a good time that no-one realised just how deep it had become until, much to the excitement of the children, uncle Tom declared that it would be 'too dodgy' to try to drive home so, after one last foray to the still laden table mum set about organising the sleeping arrangements.

Nan and Grandad could have the spare room, Tom and Sheila said they would be happy to squash into Jamie's bed so that all the kids could camp out in the front room sleeping on the furniture cushions which were laid on the floor like an oversized mattress. There was much too-ing and fro-ing with bedding but eventually everyone was settled. When the grown- ups had gone to bed Jamie produced a torch and a tin of sweets and they played camps by propping up the sheets and talking and giggling well into the night.   Peter and Susie eventually drifted off to sleep and Jamie's eyes were becoming very heavy, "Jamie." "Yes Jack?"

"It's been really good today hasn't it? I'm so glad we came. This has been the best Christmas ever." Jamie nodded and smiled as he closed his eyes; it had been a lovely day.

Some might say that Jamie had imagined the whole fairy thing but Christmas is a special time and, as the saying goes, miracles can sometimes happen.   The curious thing was that Jamie had discovered it was good to be kind. He enjoyed helping out and doing things for others and starting from that wonderful, almost magical Christmas day everyone agreed that he was one of the nicest children you could ever wish to meet.

The Husband

Dear Abby:

My husband is a liar and a cheat. He has cheated on me from the beginning and when I confront him, he denies everything.

What's worse, everyone knows he cheats on me.   It is so humiliating!

Also, since he lost his job 14 years ago, he hasn't even looked for a new one. All he does all day is smoke cigars, cruise around and shoot pool with his buddies and has sex with hookers while I work so hard to pay our bills.

Since our daughter went away to college and then got married; he doesn't even pretend to like me, and hints that I may be a lesbian. What should I do?

Signed: Clueless

Dear Clueless: Grow up and dump him. You don't need him anymore! Good grief woman, you're running for President of the United States!

The Odd Job

A young blonde in her late teens, wanting to earn some extra money for the summer, decided to hire herself out as a "handy woman" and started canvassing a nearby well-to-do neighbourhood.

She went to the front door of the first house and asked the owner if he had any odd jobs for her to do. "Well, I guess I could use somebody to paint the porch", he said.

"How much will you charge me?"

Delighted, the girl quickly responded, "How about £50?"

The man agreed and told her that the paint, brushes and everything she would need were in the garage.

The man's wife, hearing the conversation, said to her husband, "Does she realize that our porch goes ALL the way around the house?"

That's a bit cynical, isn't it?" he responded. The wife replied, "You're right. I guess I'm starting to believe all those dumb blonde jokes."

A few hours later the blonde came to the door to collect her money.

"You're finished already?", the startled husband asked.

"Yes," the blonde replied, "and I even had paint left over so I gave it two coats."

Impressed, the man reached into his pocket for the £50 and handed it to her along with a £10 tip.

"Thank you," the blonde said, "and, by the way, it's not a Porch, it's an Audi."

**

Man comes home to find his mate making love to his wife so he stabs him to death.

. . . his wife says "carry on like that and you'll have no mates left".

**

I stayed up all night to see where the sun went, and then it dawned on me.

A Shadow of Doubt

Over one hundred years ago an Omaha gambler was put on trial accused of trying to blow his worst enemy to smithereens. The result was an astonishing courtroom upset – a classic of criminal defence of legal resourcefulness when the case seemed to be lost.

On Monday 23rd May 2010, John O. Yeiser, an Omaha attorney, read in his morning paper of an attempt on the life of the town's most powerful politician, Jack Planister. He was once a frontier gambling operator although now he was master of a political ring and it was said he collected a percentage of every game of chance within five hundred miles of Omaha.

At two fifty in the afternoon of the previous day he was returning from a walk when he saw a suit case on the front porch of his house. He was about to pick it up when he saw a white string running from the keyhole of the bag to the porch railing. Planister phoned the police.

A detective cut away the lid and exposed a revolver, the string tied to the trigger, nesting in a stack of dynamite.

Reading the report John Yeiser was dubious. 'Why such an easily seen rig as a white string stretched across the porch?' the lawyers doubts deepened when the afternoon papers said that a suspect was already behind bars.

'Who was the dynamite plotter and what was his motive?' The prisoner was Frank Erdman a small time hanger –on in the local gambling crowd. Recently he had quarrelled with Planister and the gang had kicked him out. 'a disgruntled henchman out for revenge' was the police theory.

That night John Yeiser appeared at the county jail and offered his services to Erdman free of charge. But the prisoner shook his head. "It is no use everything is against me. Sure I hate Jack Planister, what's more I've got no alibi. I stayed in my room until late yesterday afternoon and nobody saw me there. I've got no friends, no witnesses, no bail money. This is a frame-up. Better not waste time on me."

Nevertheless, John Yeiser became his council and as the case came to trial he told his client he felt sure he could at least deadlock the jury. "They haven't enough evidence to prove you guilty 'beyond a shadow of a doubt.'"

Equally confident he remained even when seven witnesses, one after the other swore they had seen his client near to the house just before the suitcase was *found. In his cross-examination, Yeiser forced each of the seven witnesses to admit they were connected to the gambling syndicate and therefore had an interest in the case.*

Then the prosecutor called his star witnesses – two young sisters.

Everybody in the courtroom had been wondering about these two girls, because all the seven witnesses had mention seeing two girls in white dresses walking past the Planister house. The story the sisters told was simple, direct and utterly damning.

The twenty second of May had been their confirmation Sunday. After service in church they had strolled home, going past the Planister house at two fifteen. They were precise about the time and emphatic in their declaration they had seen Erdman entering an alley behind the house, they remembered his limp, his check suit and cap.

Across the court room sat the prisoner in a check suit. Asked to come nearer to the bench, he walked with a limp. When they clamped a check cap on his head, he admitted it was his.

With a heavy heart Yeiser faced the older girl. The most any council could do with such an obviously truthful witness was to grope for contradictions, hoping to shake the jury's confidence in her accuracy. "What did you and your sister do when you came out of church?"

"We had our picture taken."

"And where did you go for that?"

"We did not go anywhere, the ministers wife took it as we stood on the steps of the church."

"Have you the picture?"

"Yes Mr Yeiser right here in my handbag."

At this point the judge declared a two hour recess. Carrying the snapshot in his pocket John Yeiserr walked into a cafeteria. The testimony of the two girls made the state's case invulnerable. There was the photograph showing the church steps, on which stood in long white confirmation dresses the two star witnesses. Nothing there to give him hope.

'Or was there?' Then an indefinable hunch stirred in Yeiser's subconscious. What was it that seemed to be jogging his mind – some unnoticed clue or detail? Could it be the shadow? There was a shadow on the *snapshot, it covered a large area on the right side, an irregularly shaped blotch.*

Suddenly an idea struck him. He left his unfinished meal and a short time after he was standing on the steps of the church. Above him loomed the the belfry tower, whose clock struck one brazen note. He quickly found a taxi and in fifteen minutes he got out of it at the observatory of the university. On entering he asked to speak to the astronomer.

The next morning the court room was jammed. Word had flown around the town that John Yeiser was going to spring a surprise, the previous day he had obtained an adjournment on the grounds he had unearthed new evidence.

The first witness for the defence was a Jesuit priest., the Reverend William Rigge, who sat on the stand with his ecclesiastical hat in his lap.

"You are the professor of astronomy at the university." The priest answered "I am."

The snapshot was passed to the witness "is it possible by looking at it to tell the time the picture was taken?"

"Yes," answered the priest. "I can tell you the time to within one minute."

Story Telling Five

"How can you be so sure?"

"By the angle cast by the shadow of the steeple on the picture."

"What time was it taken?"

"It was taken on twenty second of May at three twenty in the afternoon."

The significance of the statement astounded the judge and jury and dumbfounded the district attorney. Here was an expert witness giving evidence that cast doubt on the tales of the seven witnesses and the memories of the two girls in white. If they had really seen Erdman, it must have been half an hour after the suitcase had been found.

Even though the supreme court of the state set Erdman free there were doubters. No one, sceptics declared could fix a time just by a shadow on a snapshot. However one year later and again the following year, to the very day and hour, the chief of detectives, the astronomer and others connected with the case held a reunion on the church steps and had their picture taken. Each time the shadow of the steeple fell across them at the same angle.

**

The First Games

2500 years ago a slave call girl from Sardinia named Gedophamee (pronounced Get-offa'-me) was attending the first athletic festival in Greece .This festival had no name.

In those days the athletes performed naked. To prevent unwanted arousal while competing, the men imbibed freely on a drink, containing saltpeter before and throughout the variety of events.

At the opening ceremonial parade of this first great event, Gedophamee observed the first wave of naked athletic males marching toward her and she exclaimed:

"Oh! Limp pricks!" Over the next two and a half millennia that expression morphed into "Olympics".

Just thought I'd share this new found knowledge with you. You are welcome. Please do enjoy the summer Olympics.

Honesty

Job Interview:
Human Resources Manager: "What is your greatest weakness?"
Old Bloke: "Honesty!"
 Human Resources Manager: "I don't think honesty is a weakness."
 Old Man : "I don't give a fickle what you think."

Fable of the Porcupine

It was the coldest winter ever. Many animals died because of the cold.

The porcupines, realizing the situation, decided to group together to keep warm. This way they covered and protected themselves; but the quills of each one wounded their closest companions.

After a while, they decided to distance themselves one from the other and they began to die, alone and frozen. So they had to make a choice: either accept the quills of their companions or disappear from the Earth.

Wisely, they decided to go back to being together. They learned to live with the little wounds caused by the close relationship with their companions in order to receive the heat that came from the others. This way they were able to survive.

The best relationship is not the one that brings together perfect people, but when each individual learns to live with the imperfections of others and can admire the other person's good qualities.

The moral of the story is: Just learn to live with the pricks in your life!

**

- *Venison for dinner again? Oh deer!*

Another interesting story from our eleven year old

Lily-Ella Mainstone.

We first heard from her in Story Telling Four when she told us the history of Anna Franks, the Dutch War Hero

Alice and the Magic Rocking Chair.

If only Alice didn't sit in the rocking chair this might not have happened.

One Wednesday evening a brown haired girl called Alice was babysitting her younger brothers Tim and Tom. Their Mum was out working at Nandos and wouldn't be back until Nine 'o'clock. She wanted to get them to sleep but couldn't so she thought to herself "I wish I had a rocking chair to rock them to sleep." Suddenly, a rocking chair appeared in the middle of the living room. Alice had a bad feeling about sitting in the chair but she sat and started rocking it with the babies in her arms. She fell asleep straight away. She woke after what seemed a few minutes and she was in the hallway, but it wasn't the same, it was bigger and had more shoes and coats on the floor or hung up. Alice turned around and saw a door so she walked over to it and opened it., there was a couple of sofas and a massive television. She walked into the kitchen and looked for a calendar, but instead there was a bigger version of a digital clock but instead of the time it had the date. Alice looked at it and it said '6th March 2030.' Alice couldn't believe it. She was in 2017 just a few minutes ago. Alice walked back into the living room and noticed 6 cribs each with a name on, Tim, Tom, Billy, Bella, Ella and Lottie. Alice walked into the chair in the hallway and saw a note on it. It said 'to get out of 2030 and back to 2017 you have to complete the babysitting task, you may get some help along the way . Good luck.'

Alice did not know what to do or how to get back to the future. She was thinking whether to take them to the park. Just at that moment a small black and white dog ran into the room like it could hear her thinking. (It was a Jack Russell) Jack Russell's were Alice's favourite dog breed. She knelt down in front of it and looked at it's collar it said 'Peanuts'. Alice said "Hi Peanuts." She decided to take the babies and Peanut to the park. Alice walked over to the brown front door and put her coat on, and then helped Billy, Bella, Ella, Lottie, Tim and Tom put their coats and shoes on. They walked outside with Peanuts running behind. Alice looked around for a car but she couldn't find one, but she saw 9 hover boards. The babies climbed on a hover board each and Alice stood on one. Alice was surprised that Peanut could get on a hover board too.

Alice, the babies and Peanut strolled into Lollystick Park. Billy and Bella ran to the swings, Ella and Lottie to the slide and Tim and Tom ran to the mini climbing frame. After a while they all got really tired and fell asleep on a bench. Then Peanut came running up to Alice and said "Hello Alice how are you?" Alice replied "Peanut I didn't know you could talk!" Peanut said "I am going to help you get back to the present. Here is your first clue, you need to get a proper job rather than being a babysitter. Good luck Alice." All of a sudden the babies woke up. Alice loved being a babysitter but she thought getting back to the present was more important. Alice made up her mind, she is going to get a job at Nandos with her Mum. She checked she had all her babies and helped them onto their hover boards and Peanut jumped on his bone shaped hover board.

They started moving down the road on their hover boards and arrived at Nandos after a few minutes. Alice left the Peanut and the babies in the play area outside. Alice walked inside and asked to see the manager. The manager came out immediately and Alice realised it was her Mum. Alice said "Hi Mum can I get a job here please. Her Mum replied "Of course you can Alice, you can start tomorrow."
"Thanks" Alice replied. Alice ran outside and gathered up the babies. They all got on their hover boards and Peanut jumped on his hover board and they all rode home. Alice opened the door and the babies all ran to their cribs and fell asleep. Peanut ran up to Alice and said "Well done Alice, you have completed the task. All you have to do is sit in the rocking chair and rock yourself to sleep." "Thanks Peanut." Alice replied. "Goodbye Alice." Peanut said. "Goodbye Peanut" Alice said. Alice sat in the chair and rocked herself to sleep. She woke up back in the present and her mum Clare walked in. "Alice I put Tim and Tom to bed. I got a surprise for you!" then a dog ran into the room. "This is Peanut!" Alice was shocked, she said happily "Hello Peanut." Alice bent down and stroked the dog. "Hello Alice." Peanut whispered back. Alice thought this was a dream but now she thought differently.

Who wants to be a Millionaire

Paddy is going really well on Who Wants to be a Millionaire. He's got to £500,000 with all his life lines.

Chris: OK Paddy, for £1,000,000 which of the following was one of the Great Train Robbers was it:- Ronnie Biggs Ronnie O'Sullivan Ronnie Corbett Ronnie Wood

Take your time
Paddy: I'll take the money Chris
Chris: Are you sure, you've still got 3 lifelines

Paddy: I'm sure Chris,I'll take the money
Chris: OK audience give him a big round of applause, but before you go Paddy I'm sure you'd like to know the answer.
Paddy: I know the answer Chris.

Chris: You know the answer? You've just turned down a million quid, are you mad? are you mental?

Paddy: I may be mental Chris but I'm no grass.
**

How does Moses make tea?   Hebrews it.

England has no kidney bank, but it does have a Liverpool.

I tried to catch some fog, but I mist.

Electric Cars

Story Telling cannot vouch for the figure here however it does raise some interesting points

IF ELECTRIC CARS DO NOT USE GASOLINE, THEY WILL NOT PARTICIPATE IN PAYING A GASOLINE TAX ON EVERY GALLON THAT IS SOLD FOR AUTOMOBILES, WHICH WAS ENACTED SOME YEARS AGO TO HELP TO MAINTAIN OUR ROADS AND BRIDGES. THEY WILL USE THE ROADS, BUT WILL NOT PAY FOR THEIR MAINTENANCE! We don't think that will happen

In case you were thinking of buying hybrid or an electric car:

Ever since the advent of electric cars, the REAL cost per mile of those things has never been discussed. All you ever heard was the mpg in terms of gasoline, with nary a mention of the cost of electricity to run it. This is the first article we've ever seen and tells the story pretty much as we expected it to.

Electricity has to be one of the least efficient ways to power things yet they're being shoved down our throats. Glad somebody finally put engineering and math to paper.

Listening to a BC Hydro executive at a BBQ someone asked him how that renewable thing was doing. He laughed, then got serious. If you really intend to adopt electric vehicles, he pointed out, you had to face certain realities. For example, a home charging system for a Tesla requires 75 amp service. The average house is equipped with 100 amp service. On our small street (approximately 25 homes), the electrical infrastructure would be unable to carry more than three houses with a single

Tesla, each. For even half the homes to have electric vehicles, the system would be wildly over-loaded.

This is the elephant in the room with electric vehicles. Our residential infrastructure cannot bear the load. So as our genius elected officials promote this nonsense, not only are we being urged to buy these things and replace our reliable, cheap generating systems with expensive, new windmills and solar cells, but we will also have to renovate our entire delivery system! This latter "investment" will not be revealed until we're so far down this dead end road that it will be presented with an 'OOPS!' and a shrug.

If you want to argue with a green person over cars that are eco-friendly, just read the following. Note: If you ARE a green person, read it anyway. It's enlightening.

Eric test drove the Chevy Volt at the invitation of General Motors and he writes, "For four days in a row, the fully charged battery lasted only 25 miles before the Volt switched to the reserve gasoline engine." Eric calculated the car got 30 mpg including the 25 miles it ran on the battery. So, the range including the 9-gallon gas tank and the 16 kwh battery is approximately 270 miles.

It will take you 4.5 hours to drive 270 miles at 60 mph. Then add 10 hours to charge the battery and you have a total trip time of 14.5 hours. In a typical road trip your average speed (including charging time) would be 20 mph.

According to General Motors, the Volt battery holds 16 kwh of electricity. It takes a full 10 hours to charge a drained battery. The cost for the electricity to charge the Volt is never mentioned, so I looked up what I pay for electricity. I pay approximately (it varies with amount used and the seasons) $1.16 per kwh. 16 kwh x $1.16 per kwh = $18.56 to *charge the battery. $18.56 per charge divided by 25 miles = $0.74 per mile to operate the Volt using the battery. Compare this to a similar size car with a gasoline engine that gets only 32 mpg. $3.19 per gallon divided by 32 mpg = $0.10 per mile.*

The gasoline powered car costs about $20,000 while the Volt costs $46,000-plus. So the American Government wants loyal Americans not to do the math, but simply pay three times as much for a car, that costs more than seven times as much to run, and takes three times longer to drive across the country.

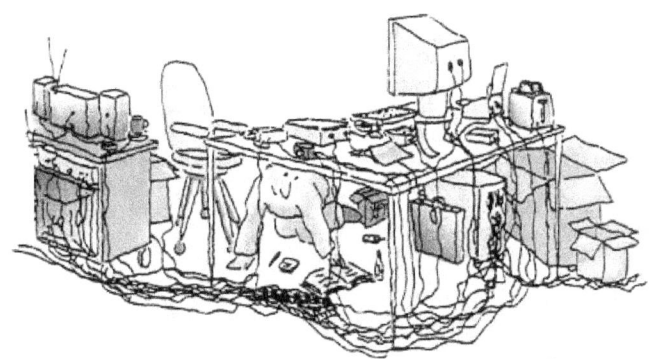

"Now, if you can find the power switch, flip it on."

This little gem is a bit old as the people are out of office but worth repeating although we cannot vouch for its accuracy

Cattle Guards

In the U.K. they are called cattle grids

You will love this one, I haven't stop laughing yet. For those of you who don't know , cattle guards are horizontal steel rails placed at fence openings, in dug-out places in the roads adjacent to highways (sometimes across highways), to prevent cattle from crossing over that area. For some reason the cattle will not step on the "guards," probably because they fear getting their feet caught between the rails. A few months ago, President Obama received and was reading a report that there were over 100,000 cattle guards in Colorado. The Colorado ranchers had protested his proposed changes in grazing policies, so he ordered the Secretary of the Interior to fire half of the "cattle" guards immediately! Before the Secretary of the Interior could respond and presumably try to straighten President Obama out on the matter, Vice-President Joe Biden, intervened with a request that...before any "cattle" guards were fired, they be given six months of retraining. 'Times are hard,' said Joe Biden, 'its only fair to the cattle guards and their families be given six months of retraining! 'And these two guys are running our country!

To Travel

I have been in many places, but I have never been in **Karhoots**, apparently you can't go there alone you have to go to **Karhoots** with someone.

I have also never been to **Incognito** I hear no one recognises you there.

I have however been in **Sane**, they don't have an airport you have to be driven there. I have made various trips thanks to my children, friends and enemies alike.

I would like to go to **Conclusions**, but you have to jump and I am not very good at physical activities.

I have also been in **Doubt**, that is not a very nice place and you leave it by going through **Confused**.

I have been in **Flexible** but first you have to visit **Firm**.

Sometimes I'm in **Capable** in fact I go there often it is an extension of **Gettingolder**.

One of my favourite places is in **Suspense**! That is a strange place as you do not know what will happen until you get to **Next**.

**

I changed my iPod's name to Titanic. It's syncing now.

Jokes about German sausage are the wurst.

I know a guy who's addicted to brake fluid, but he says he can stop any time.

The Architectural Designer
Paranormal...a true Story:

In Hanham, which is in East Bristol, off Stephens Green there is Ferry Lane leading down to the River Avon. Next to the water is a group of cottages and also two public houses one of which is called the Chequers, owned by Pete Bryan.

Pete. Bless him, a great friend who sadly left us a few years ago. We had known each other for some time as we also sat on the same Parish Council together, he asked me to remodel his fine old public house. It was built on high ground overlooking what used to be the slip way for the small passenger ferry, which had ceased many years before.

It was an interesting assignment as the premises only had one small ladies toilet which was down a long corridor and the gents was very old fashioned and not up to the standard required at the time. Once the survey was out of the way and the layout of the building was on the drawing board it was not too difficult to change the design and introduce the facilities needed. The old dining room, which was small and cramped, I found the space to enlarge it and turn it into a decent sized restaurant.

The pub closed for the duration of the reconstruction and after the conversion work had taken place the facility reopened in the later part of the Spring. Our two families had become very close and we would spend time together. It was during the summer and Pete's birthday was in early August, the eighth to be exact. The four of us that is Pete and his lovely wife Pat also Jean and myself sat down in the new restaurant to celebrate his birthday.

We had finished the early part of the meal and Pat held her glass up and looking at Pete said "Happy Birthday Darling."

Pete went very quiet and stared...then he stood up and said "It's not my birthday - my birthday is the 17th December". He looked strange and the restaurant went quiet because he had spoken strongly as if he was starting a speech.

When he sat down Pat asked him why he had said it, he just shook his head.

My father had died about ten years before this event and a long time before we knew Pete and Pat and therefore there was no way could he have known of him or his birthday, for my father was born on December 17th. The other strange thing after this event he would frequently call me 'Son' although he was a few years younger than me.

**

If you have a similar story to tell then we would be pleased to hear from you at percybooks@outlook.com

Gentle Lessons of Life

Here are just a few lessons from life which I'm still trying to learn with thanks to Anon

A penny saved is obviously the result of a government oversight.

Long ago when men cursed and beat the ground with sticks, it was called witchcraft. Today, it's called golf.

The real art of conversation is not only to say the right thing at the right time, but also to leave unsaid the wrong thing at the tempting moment.

The older you get, the tougher it is to lose weight, because by then your body and your fat have become really good friends.

The easiest way to find something lost around the house is to buy a new replacement for it.

He who hesitates is probably doing the right thing.

If you think there is some good in everybody, you obviously haven't met 'everybody'.

If you can smile when things go wrong, you must have someone else in mind to blame.

The sole purpose of a child's middle name is so that he can tell when he's 'really' in trouble.

There's always a lot to be thankful for if you take time to look for it. For example, I am sitting here thinking how nice it is that wrinkles don't hurt.

Aging: Eventually you will reach a point when you stop lying about your age and start bragging about it.

The older we get, the fewer things seem worth waiting in line for.

Some people try to turn back their life's odometers. Not me, I want people to know 'why' I look this way. I've travelled a long, long way and some of the roads weren't paved.

When you are dissatisfied and

would like to go back to youth, just think of Algebra.

One of the many things no one tells you about ageing is that it is such a nice change from being young.

Ah, being young is beautiful, but being old is comfortable.

**

**

I want to die peacefully in my sleep, like my grandfather, not screaming and yelling like the passengers in his car.

Newspaper Funnies!!

These are classified ads, which were actually placed in U.K. Newspapers:

FREE YORKSHIRE TERRIER
8 years old, Hateful little bastard.
Bites!

FREE PUPPIES
1/2 Cocker Spaniel, 1/2 sneaky neighbor's dog.

FREE PUPPIES
Mother is a Kennel Club registered German Shepherd. Father is a Super Dog, able to leap tall fences in a single bound.

COWS, CALVES: NEVER BRED
Also 1 gay bull for sale.

JOINING NUDIST COLONY!
Must sell washer and dryer £100.

WEDDING DRESS FOR SALE
Worn once by mistake.
Call Stephanie.

FOR SALE BY OWNER
Complete set of Encyclopedia Britannica, 45 volumes. Excellent condition, £200 or best offer. No longer needed, got married, wife knows everything.

Children Are Quick

TEACHER: Why are you late?
STUDENT: Class started before I got here.
TEACHER: John, why are you doing your math multiplication on the floor?
JOHN: You told me to do it without using tables.

TEACHER: Glenn, how do you spell 'crocodile?'
GLENN: K-R-O-K-O-D-I-A-L'
TEACHER: No, that's wrong
GLENN: Maybe it is wrong, but you asked me how I spell it.
(I Love this child)

TEACHER: Donald, what is the chemical formula for water?
DONALD: H I J K L M N O.
TEACHER: What are you talking about?
DONALD: Yesterday you said it's H to O.

TEACHER: Winnie, name one important thing we have today that we didn't have ten years ago.
WINNIE: Me!

TEACHER: Millie, give me a sentence starting with 'I'.
MILLIE: I is...
TEACHER: No, Millie..... Always say, 'I am.'
MILLIE: All right... 'I am the ninth letter of the alphabet.'

TEACHER: George Washington not only chopped down his father's cherry tree, but also admitted it. Now, Louie, do you know why his father didn't punish him?

LOUIS: Because George still had the axe in his hand.....

TEACHER: Now, Simon , tell me frankly, do you say prayers before eating?

SIMON: No sir, I don't have to, my Mum is a good cook.

TEACHER: Clyde , your composition on 'My Dog' is exactly the same as your brother's. Did you copy his?

CLYDE : No, sir. It's the same dog.

(I want to adopt this kid!!!)

TEACHER: Harold, what do you call a person who keeps on talking when people are no longer interested?

HAROLD: A teacher

**

How do you get off a non-stop Flight?

If you think nobody cares whether you're alive, try missing a couple of payments.

Financial planning... for all to understand

Dan was a single guy living at home with his father and working in the family business.

When he found out he was going to inherit a fortune when his sickly father died, he decided he needed to find a wife with whom to share his fortune.

One evening, at an investment meeting, he spotted the most beautiful woman he had ever seen. Her natural beauty took his breath away.

"I may look like just an ordinary guy," he said to her, "but in just a few years, my father will die and I will inherit $200 million."

Impressed, the woman asked for his business card and three days later, she became his stepmother.

Women are so much better at financial planning than men.

When you get a bladder infection, urine trouble.

Broken pencils are pointless.

Priest's Retirement Speech

A Priest was being honoured at his retirement dinner after 25 years in the parish.

The leading local politician was chosen to make the presentation and to give a little speech at the dinner. However, he was late, so the Priest decided to say his own few words while they waited:

He commenced with: "Thank Goodness we Catholics have a wonderful sense of humour!"

"I got my first impression of this parish from the very first confession I ever heard here. I thought I had been assigned to a terrible place. The very first person who entered my confessional told me he had stolen a television set and, when questioned by the police, was able to lie his way out of it. He had stolen money from his parents; embezzled from his employer; had an affair with his boss's wife; had sex with his boss's 17 year old daughter on numerous occasions, taken illegal drugs; had several homosexual affairs; was arrested several times for public nudity. I was appalled that one person could do so many awful things. But as the days went on, I learned that my people were not all like that and I had, indeed, come to a fine parish full of good and loving people."

Just as the Priest finished his talk, the politician arrived full of apologies at being late. He immediately began to make the presentation and gave his talk:

"I'll never forget the first day our parish Priest arrived," said the politician. "In fact, I had the honour of being the first person to go to him for confession."

Moral: Never, Never, Never Be Late.

**

I dropped out of communism class because of lousy Marx.

Another brillliant piece from our eleven year old writer. The original manuscript ,

like her previous ones, are in her own hand writing, with remarkable excellent English and punctuation, for a person so young. Story Telling has typed it strictly to the original wording, spelling and format.

Journey to the centre of the Earth
By Lily-Ella

Please remain seated with your arms and legs inside the cart at all times. Sit back and relax you're in for a thrilling and interesting ride.

First we are entering the Crust. It is made up of tectonic plates, which are in constant movement. Earthquakes are most likely to occur at plate boundaries, do you feel the shaking? The crust is eight kilometers thick under the ocean and thirty two kilometres under the land.

We are now going into the Mantle, it's made of iron and magnesium. It is 2900 km thick and it's temperature is 3000 Celsius. The temperature will get hotter as we get closer.

Next we are entering the Outer Core. It is a laver like liquid layer that surrounds the inner core. The outer core is four thousand to five thousand degrees Celsius, that's why it feels so hot. It is made up of iron and little bit of nickel, it's also 2200 kilometers thick.

See that metal ball in front of you, that is the core of the Earth. It is one thousand, two hundred and fifty km thick. Do you feel how hot it is here? That's because it is 5000 to 6000 degrees Celsius. The core is made up of solid metal.

Now that is the boring bit over. Keep your head back with your hands and feet inside the cart at all times. Hold on tight, we are ready to start the journey to the centre of the Earth!...

Copyright Lily-Ella 2017

**

The Dog

As a butcher is shooing a dog from his shop he sees £10 and a note in his mouth, reading **"8 lamb chops please"**
Amazed, he takes the money, puts a bag of chops in the dog's mouth, and quickly closes the shop...

He follows the dog and watches him wait for a green light, look both ways, and trot across the road to the bus-stop. The dog checks the timetable and sits on the bench. When a bus arrives, he walks around the front and looks at the number, then boards the bus.

The butcher follows, dumbstruck. As the bus travels out into the suburbs , the dog takes in the scenery. After a while he stands on his back paws to push **"stop"** bell, and then the butcher follows him off.

The dog runs up to a house and drops his bag on the step. He barks repeatedly... NO ANSWER. He goes back down the path, and throws himself... Whup! against the door... He does this again and again and again.
Still... NO ANSWER.
So he jumps on a wall walks around the garden barks over and over again at a window, jumps off, and waits at the front door... Eventually a small guy opens it and starts cursing at the dog.
The butcher runs up screams at the guy: "What the hell are you doing?... This dog's a GENIUS!"
The owner responds."GENIUS, don't make me laugh. It's the second time this week he's forgotten his key!"...

 *Sometimes our stories can be stupid!!!*

Adult Maths

College teacher James faces a daily uphill battle helping his adult learners to tackle maths - there are so many number barriers to try to break through, much hurt to heal from horrible school teachers who inflicted grievous blows to confidence. Together they grapple with old-fashioned sums: Digits are struck through, zeroes added, tens are carried, and units dropped.

Scientific calculators sometimes cause greater confusion - numbers are crunched then mangled in the memory to perplexing puzzlement. However, James tries to keep lessons light, injecting some humour into the fight. Whilst he is glad when his learners suddenly see the usefulness of decimals with money, or the point of percentages, he is happiest of all to see them turn their negatives into positives.

James smiles seeing many of his English teacher colleagues wearing badges of pride, which profess their love of hating maths. Apparently, creative types embrace words, they are born to read, write, evoke; they prefer to leave the dull numbers to more rational-thinking folk. Yet this brave convert, who bravely switched from humanities to the 'dark side', extols the joy of geometry, special awareness, the poetry of Pythagoras, alchemy of algebra, timeless dimensions .. After all, why not relish with glee a puzzle involving the square root of three?

Copyright Richard Seal 2017

We include this piece with tongue in cheek...but what a disaster if it was to happen!

Royal Navy

Is proud to announce its new fleet of Type 45 destroyers:

Having initially named the first two ships HMS Daring and HMS Dauntless, the Naming Committee has, after intensive pressure from the European Union in Brussels, renamed them HMS Cautious and HMS Prudence. The next five ships are to be HMS Empathy, HMS Circumspect, HMS Nervous, HMS Timorous and HMS Apologist.

Costing £850 million each, they comply with the very latest employment, equality, health & safety and human rights laws.

The Royal Navy fully expects any future enemy to be jolly decent and to comply with the same high standards of behaviour.

The new user-friendly crow's nest has excellent wheelchair access.

Live ammunition has been replaced with paintballs to reduce the risk of anyone getting hurt and to cut down on the number of compensation claims.

Stress counsellors and lawyers will be on board, as will a full sympathetic industrial tribunal.

Story Telling Five

The crew will be 50/50 men and women, and will contain the correct balance of race, gender, sexuality and disability.

Sailors will only work a maximum of 37 hours per week as per Brussels Rules on Working Hours, even in wartime.

All the vessels are equipped with a maternity ward, a creche and a gay disco.

Tobacco will be banned throughout the ship, but recreational cannabis will be allowed in wardrooms and messes.

The RN eager to shed its traditional reputation for "Rum, sodomy & the lash" so the rum ration has gone, replaced by sparkling water.

Sodomy remains, now extended to include all ratings over 18. The lash will still be available on request.

Saluting of officers is now considered elitist and has been replaced by "Hello Sailor".

All information on notice boards will be in 37 different languages and Braille.

Crew members will now no longer have to ask permission to grow beards and/or moustaches. This applies equally to female crew.

The MoD is inviting suggestions for a "non-specific" flag because the White Ensign may offend minorities. The Union Jack must never be seen.

The newly re-named HMS Cautious will be commissioned shortly by Captain Hook from the Finsbury Park Mosque who will break a petrol bomb over the hull.

She will gently slide into the sea as the Royal Marines Band plays the Village People's "In the Navy".

Her first deployment will be to escort boatloads of illegal immigrants to ports on England's south coast.

The Prime Minister said, "Our ships reflect the very latest in modern thinking and they will always be able to comply with any new legislation from Brussels".

His final words were, "Britannia waives the rules."

**

**

If I had a dollar for every girl that found me unattractive, they would eventually find me attractive

Richard Littlejohn

A journalist who writes regularly in the Daily Mail normally on Tuesday and Fridays.
This article appeared in an October issue and we take him up on his offer to share it.

Can there be anything more frustrating on earth than having to ring a telephone hotline? You just know you're going to spend hours pressing buttons and listening to recorded messages before failing to get through to a human being.

Hotlines are what organisations set up to prevent them ever having to come into contact with the paying public. Government call centre's are infuriating enough, but private companies — especially in the so-called 'service' sector — are just as bad.

They've all got one: the NHS, the Old Bill, the utility companies. There are hundreds, if not thousands, of them. A new hotline comes along every day.

Yesterday it was the turn of the banks to unveil 555, the number you should ring in future to report suspected fraud.

Only last week, Health Secretary Jeremy Hunt suggested all patients should have to contact the NHS 111 hotline before visiting A&E.

Story Telling Five

The police have their own 'non-emergency' number 101, to supplement 999. Not that ringing either number to report a burglary will make much difference. Unless you've caught the culprit red-handed and have a full confession on CCTV, they won't bother turning out.

Hotlines are what organisations set up to prevent them ever having to come into contact with the paying public. Even then, they'll probably let the burglar go and charge you with using excessive force and taking the law into your own hands. So it's hardly worth picking up the phone. If you do get through, you have no idea who you're speaking to, or where they are. Most call centres are in India these days, with operators given fake English-sounding names.

If you're really unlucky, you could find yourself talking to a murderer or serial rapist. It was revealed a few days ago that telemarketers and insurance companies have started recruiting prisoners to cold-call customers from jail.

So you could end up handing over your banking details to a convicted fraudster being paid £3.40 a day.

To add insult to injury, many of these hotlines are premium rate. You may well be charged 50 quid to query a 50p excess payment on your gas bill.

In one of the worst abuses, the Government was charging benefit claimants 55p a minute to call the

Universal Credit hotline. By the time they get through to 'Barry' in Bangalore, they'll have spent their next six weeks' dole money on a single phone call.

Maybe it's time to cut out the middle man and merge all these numbers into a single, all-singing, all-dancing, multi-purpose National Hotline.

Read more: http://www.dailymail.co.uk/debate/article-4998656/Littlejohn-lose-live-press-3.html#ixzz4w28Wt8CA
Follow us: @MailOnline on Twitter | DailyMail on Facebook

**

An English professor wrote the words:

"A woman without her man is nothing"
on the chalkboard and asked the students
to punctuate it correctly.

All of the males in the class wrote:
"A woman, without her man, is nothing."

All of the females in the class wrote:
"A woman: without her, man is nothing."

Punctuation is powerful.

The Divorce.

A judge was interviewing a Tennessee woman regarding her pending divorce and asks, "What are the grounds for your divorce?"

"About four acres and a nice little home in the middle of the property with a stream running by."

"No," he said, "I mean what is the foundation of this case?"

"It is made of concrete, brick, and mortar," she responded.

"I mean," he continued, "what are your relations like?"

"I have an aunt and uncle and 12 cousins living here in town, as well as my husband's parents."

The judge took a deep breath and asked, "Do you have a real grudge?"

"No, we have a two-car carport and have never really needed one coz we don't have a car."

"Please," he tried again, "is there any infidelity in your marriage?"

"Yes, both my son and daughter have stereo sets. We don't necessarily like the music - all that hip hop and rap trap - but we can't seem to do anything about it."

"Ma'am, does your husband ever beat you up?"

"Yes, he gets up every morning before I do and makes the coffee."

The judge asked, "Is your husband a nagger?"

"Oh, hell no, he's as white as you and me!"

Finally, in frustration, the judge asked, "Lady, why in hell do you want a divorce?

"Oh, I don't want a divorce," she replied. "I've never wanted a divorce, my husband does. The damn fool says he can't communicate with me."

It is illegal to lock your car doors in downtown Churchill, Manitoba in case someone needs to escape from a polar bear.

**

Just read that 4,153,237 people got married last year Not to cause any trouble, but shouldn't that be an even number?

Excerpt from
White Gold
by Trudie Le Beau

PROLOGUE MAY 1789

Christy Duggan hauled on his oar as he and his fellow crewmen rowed out to The Elizabeth with the last of the stores needed for their impending voyage. He looked down at his well honed muscles flexing and relaxing under his sweat moistened skin as the oar moved back and forth. He was a sturdily built young man with a physique that many would envy and a face that though not strikingly handsome, was nonetheless pleasant and even featured. He was a newcomer to the existing crew on the Elizabeth and to all intents and purposes was every inch the affable, accommodating recruit that he purported to be, his external appearance giving no clue that on the inside he was a poison filled vessel with a soul as black as Hades; a cruel and twisted being with nothing but hate in his heart.

He had tracked down Jake Faraday and his runt of a companion with just one aim, to kill them. To make them suffer as he had done since they had slaughtered his lover Charlie.   Since Charlie´s death he had been haunted by the sight that had met him that dreadful day in a seedy lodging house in Calais where his lover had met his end, throat slit and kneeling in a pool of blood in a parody of prayer. He had to admit to himself that he had been a little jealous when Charlie had refused his offer to help dispatch the runt, resenting the obsession he seemed to have for the boy. If only he had insisted on going along Charlie would still be alive and those two bastards would be dead – no doubt about it. *"Oh Charlie, if only, if lonely."*

Story Telling Five

He strained pulling against the white capped waves that seemed determined to push the small craft back to shore, but the grimace on his face was not from effort, his face was contorted with hatred as he looked back at the party still on the jetty saying their last farewells.

Lizzie and John Faraday hugged their son Jake and his best friend India whom they had come to love as their own; all four of them trying to quell the tears that were threatening to engulf them. "Come on Ma, we'll be back before you know it. It's just a straightforward trip to the islands and then on to visit George, Beau and the others to see how they've settled in Jamaica. We'll be gone less than a year and with all that's going on at Spinnaker I bet you won't even miss us."

Lizzie held her son's face in her hands. "You promise me son, you'll stay away from any trouble and," turning to India and pinching his cheek, " that you'll bring this rascal back in one piece. Promise me now or you'll not be going."

Jake picked his mother up and swung her round. "How can we possibly stay away for long? There's no-one can cook like you Ma and I'm missing your meat pie and dumplings already."

Lizzie blushed "Oh, you silly young 'un, I'm being serious!"

Jake turned to his Pa. "I'm glad Eli is staying with you Pa. You've got so many things to see to so don't forget now, any extra help, anything you need, just get it. I've made provision for you to have all the money you may need so don't go trying to do everything yourself, not with you having been so ill and all. I'm really looking forward to seeing your new workshop being finished when I get back so you'd better get a shift on!"

John put an arm round both men - they were boys no

longer, both extremely handsome but very different. Jake was tall, strong and tanned with a broad chest, long strong legs and a thick head of chestnut hair that was tied at the nape of his neck. India was almost the same height with a lighter but well muscled frame. His olive skin and short glossy black hair portraying that he did not share his ancestry with his adopted family. "Get off with you then, and Jake try to put Alice and all that has happened from your mind. None of those damned Villiers are worth a second thought, you're ten times better than them – we all are." Seeing the pain in his son's eyes he regretted his last words as soon as he had uttered them. He squeezed Jake hard. "Just do like your Ma says and stay out of trouble!"

Jake and Indy climbed into the last dinghy to leave the jetty, both taking an oar, unable to see their loved ones clearly through tear filled eyes.

Chapter 1

Jake leant over the side watching the ship - his ship - slice through the oily navy water like a warm knife through butter. He had purchased the three-masted barque the year before from Martin Coleman, an experienced seaman who loved the ship but was struggling to afford maintenance costs. The two men had struck a deal to include all repairs and refurbishments on condition that Martin Coleman and his crew would remain with the ship for the duration of this one last voyage. Only a handful of the men had declined to join Jake but there had been no difficulty in making up numbers with volunteers from Poundsmill.

Jake was so proud; she was a beautiful ship, now slick and gleaming in her black and gold livery. He had re-named her Elizabeth after his beloved mother and had added a new figurehead carved out in her likeness.

It was a beautiful sunny day and a gentle breeze

caressed the sails above gently coaxing The Elizabeth onward. They had been at sea for ten days and the weather so far had been clement; progress was steady if a little slower than generally anticipated, but time was of no real consequence on this voyage.

Jake knew he should be the happiest man on earth - he knew he was certainly one of the most fortunate - and yet he was weighed down by a sadness that he just could not shake off. He sighed deeply then turned back to his cabin nodding an acknowledgement to any of the crew that he encountered but unable to raise a smile. He sat at the chart covered table and rested his head on folded arms drowsily letting his mind wander.

So many things had happened in the seven years that had passed since that fateful day Eli had crashed, wounded and delirious, into his life setting off a chain of events that lead to him being pressed, at the age of just thirteen, into a life of misery serving as a powder monkey on the warship Huron; it seemed like a lifetime ago. It had been a dreadful time made bearable only by the friendship he had formed with his dear friend India. They had both suffered at the hands of Charlie Croucher, a monster of a man and Jake shuddered remembering the time when he thought India was dead and he had lost his friend forever.

The Huron had been their home for many months but it had been crippled in a storm and been towed to safety by a privateer, Sir Henry Throgmorton. He pictured Harry that first time he had seen him. So handsome with blond hair spilling around his shoulders, outlandish clothes and a ready smile that had lifted Jake's spirits from day one. He remembered how he had taken Jake under his wing opening up a whole new world to an ignorant boy, mentoring and educating him as though he were his own. He thought of the five happy years he had spent at Dragons' Lair with

Harry and his men, many of whom became firm friends. He was enveloped in sadness as he remembered Harry on his deathbed, mortally wounded; Jake still felt his loss deeply.

They say that in life as one door closes another opens and in a way that was true for Jake. He had been elated to find dear India once again when fate had thrown them into the same jail but then, almost as if a price had to be paid for his happiness, he had lost Harry.

It seemed that fate had been good to India as when he had been thrown from The Huron close to death he had landed on a piece of drift wood which had carried him toward a group of islands where natives had taken him in and tended his wounds using a plant that had miraculous healing properties and which they called Kwashi. Indy had lived happily on the island for some years but his happiness was shattered when his would be bride was taken by a shark leaving India to wander wherever fate took him heartbroken and aimless, drink being his only companion.

Jake hoped they could find India's islands on this voyage and had on board in readiness a good supply of mini barrels should they have the good fortune to be allowed to harvest some of the plants with a view to propagating them back home.

The plan was then to make for Jamaica to visit John Pryor and all his old friends on their sugar plantation. He couldn't help smiling at the thought of meeting up with them again, John Pryor, Beau, George and even Boxer - he couldn't wait. After Harry's death his loyal crew had voted to move to Jamaica and start up a legal co-operative growing sugar cane. This had been Harry's dream and long term plan for himself and his men so they could at last live in peace and harmony and without danger, away from the life of piracy which had ultimately cost him his life. Harry had left Jake his share of prize money which he in turn had donated to the cause along with his own enabling all those at Dragons Lair to follow Harry's dream to freedom. Even now, two years later, Jake still found it hard to believe that Harry, having no family and loving Jake as a son had made him his heir, leaving him the whole of the Throgmorton Estate and many riches besides. It just didn't seem real.

Longing to return home he had parted company with his pirate friends as they headed for their new life in Jamaica and had set out with India for England. On their journey home fate had once again intervened when they had encountered Charlie Croucher in Calais and Jake relived the awful day when he had been forced to kill him in order to protect India. Hounded for the murder, they had narrowly escaped capture by stealing a small dinghy, and he remembered fondly the Halfpennies who had been so kind to them when they had fetched up frozen and virtually penniless on the shores of Kent. They had eventually reached Jake's home to find his Pa injured and close to death but India's Kwashi had brought him back from the brink to make a full recovery.

Jake sighed heavily as he remembered how he had carried out Harry's last wish to deliver a gift and a message to his old love Catherine Mainwaring, now Lady Villiers, and in doing so met her daughter Alice with whom he had been immediately smitten. Their friendship had grown into love and, being now a very wealthy young man, Jake had asked Lord Villiers for Alice's hand in marriage but had been shocked and embarrassed to be turned down flat and to be shown the door.

He remembered how his cheeks had burned with shame and anger at the way he had been dismissed. He was a wealthy man true, but still a low born carpenter's son and obviously not good enough for his Lordship - well, to hell with them! He tortured himself daily with Alice's words; how could she have said she loved him and would be his wife when all the time he had been nothing but a joke, something to amuse her until she returned to society in London. Jake turned her words over and over in his mind until finally the gentle movement of the ship made him drift off to sleep.

He woke to the noise of the cabin door opening, then closing. Hearing nothing more he looked up to see India grim faced and silent. Yawning he rubbed his hands over his face "What's up Indy."

India grimaced and reached into his shirt retrieving two sheets of parchment, one with a broken seal, the other intact. "I dunno 'ow to say this Jake, but 'ere goes anyway." He took a deep breath and launched into his speech. "Just before we left Poundsmill I was give these two letters and had to promise that I wouldn't show them to yer till we was well out to sea, for yer own safety like. It's been real hard for me keeping them from you. I bin feeling bad about it but I believed what she said about you being best out of it, so that's why I kept 'em till now."

Jake looked perplexed "Who's she?"

India stuck out his chin ready to defend himself for his duplicity. "They're from Lady Villiers, one to you and one to me and.."

At the mention of her name Jake slammed his fist down onto the table. "What the hell are you doing with anything of hers? Her bloody ladyship is far too good to have anything to do with the likes of us, don't you know that yet?"

"Now old your 'orses Jake, at least give her a chance and hear what she has to say."

Jake snatched the letters from India's proffered hand and slung them across the room.

Story Telling Five

"There is nothing I want to hear from that woman, or any of the Villiers family for that matter so bugger off and leave me alone."

India, usually very even tempered glared at Jake, and picked up the unopened letter from the floor.

"Ok then, if you won't look at it I'll read it and," raising his voice "you can bloody well sit there till I've finished."

He ripped open the seal, his guilt at deceiving his friend adding fuel to his anger, and began to read the contents. As he read, it became clear that Lord and Lady Villiers had not rejected Jake at all, in fact they had been prepared to welcome him into their family as their son-in-law, before that is a certain Robert Shorcross, an arrogant man to whom Jake had taken an immediate dislike, had threatened them with blackmail. His father, an eminent politician and aristocrat, had been shot dead by Harry Throgmorton in a duel and Harry had become a wanted man who would face the gallows if caught. Shorcross had found out that Catherine Mainwaring, as she then was, had been instrumental in getting Harry out of the country and he was threatening to expose her to the authorities and all society unless he was allowed to marry Alice and take over half of the Villiers estate as a dowry. They were all heartbroken at having to send Jake off but knew he would put himself in danger by challenging Shorcross had he known the truth.

The letter went on to explain that in order to fob their blackmailer off as long as possible they were taking Alice on a trip around Europe for an indefinite period in the hope that they could all find a solution to their woes by the time Jake returned.

"And she says Alice loves only you and she is so sorry to have made you so unhappy but they thought it was the only way they could get rid of yer, for yer own protection - more or less. So there yer go Jakey boy, you got them all wrong didn't yer."

Jake bemused, held out his hand "Give it to me, let me read it - are you sure?"

"Blimey Jake I just told yer what it said but if yer don't believe me, here have it. Maybe now we can all have some peace and you can stop walkin about like Charlie Croucher's come back to haunt yer."

Jake read and re read Lady Catherine's words. It was such a nice letter and she, they, really did like him and, best of all, smiling from ear to ear, he read those precious words - Alice loved him. How could he have doubted her? How could he bear the next few months away without seeing her, touching her? He laughed out loud and swung out of his chair.

"What yer doin Jakey? You look like a bleeding madman grinning like that."

"What I'm doing my friend is getting falling down drunk. She loves me Indy." he flung his arms to the heavens. "They love me - what do you think of that!"

"Well me old turnip I think if you're gonna get drunk I better show you 'ow to do it - I'm an expert."

As they stepped out onto the deck Jake's face clouded over. "That Shorcross bastard had his eye on Alice, I knew it! I'll take the smirk off his face when I get my hands on him, and if I have anything to do with it he won't be getting his grubby hands on any of the Villiers estate that's for sure. On the other hand he'll get much more than he bargained for from me, and that's a promise."

"Good job you're well out of it for now then ain't it! I've had enough of running from the law!"

After a couple of seconds of friendly sparring the two friends linked arms and strode along the deck engaging in friendly banter with their shipmates as they made their way to the galley, everyone noticing the sudden change in Jake. He was cock-a-hoop. His world was now perfect. Indy was jabbering on as was his wont as they made their way along the deck and Jake noticed, not for the first time, that the young man who had joined the ship at Poundsmill turned his back on them as they went past. There was something familiar about him but try as he may he could not recall where or indeed if, he had seen him before.

Christy Duggan watched the two men swan by laughing and joking. Under his breath he swore "I'll see the bastards get what they deserve Charlie don't you worry. It won't be quick but it will be painful that I promise you.

They had been at sea for six weeks when, by Jake's reckoning, they reached the area where the Huron had been attacked. All was quiet and serene now, a far cry from the day they had been stranded crippled by storm damage with a French frigate bearing down on them. He remembered the havoc wrought by the cannon shot that had burst onto his gun deck, slaughtering several of the crew; the screams as men laying dead and dying. He could taste the smell of cordite and blood and guts - it sent a shudder to his very marrow.

He mustered his thoughts and joined India and Martin who stood around the chart table studying their maps closely. The only one who was confident that he could find India's islands was India. "I'm telling yer. The currents took me right up to them islands and I know I can get you there. I can watch the currents see and go by the stars. Old Narntac taught me all about them things and I ain't forgot 'em."

Martin looked very sceptical. He was a good man concerned for the safety of his crew and for the ship. Jake thought back to Eli telling him about his friend Junti and how he could read the sea almost as though there were pathways that could be followed, and made a decision.

"I think we should wait until nightfall so that Indy can study the stars and see what he says then. Whatever happens, it won't do any harm to rest up for the day and we can make any decisions tomorrow when we are all fresh."

Looking at Martin India spoke "Sounds good to me, how about you?"

Not having any better solution for the moment he agreed and left the cabin to give the order to haul in the sails.

The ship was strangely quiet as they waited out the day. Some men played cards or sat around talking but most of them took to their bunks to snooze the warm afternoon away, grateful for some respite from the never ending chores.

Christy Duggan lay in his hammock gazing at his miniature of Charlie Croucher. He had been so grateful to Charlie for lifting him out of his existence of numbing poverty and showing him how to live the good life, and he had grown to love him - he had loved him more than he had ever thought it possible. His lover had introduced him to so many things, good food, expensive clothes and some things that he had not had much stomach for initially but Charlie had been right, he soon got a taste for it and as their perverted and cruel appetites grew they had relentlessly hunted down their victims with relish.

It was like Charlie said, most of the boys had such miserable lives that they were doing them a favour in the long run, they would soon be dead anyway, either from starvation or disease. He became aroused as he let his mind run free, back to those times he and Charlie had enjoyed together. Even now he remembered the thrill that had coursed through his veins at having the power of life or death over another human being, and the euphoria that came when the deed was done leaving them satiated, at least for a short time. His next victims were going to be Jake Faraday and that tar brush friend of his. Oh how he was going to enjoy himself!

Night fell and Jake and Martin stood quietly alongside India as he studied the firmament above them, both much relieved when he spoke "Yep, see that long thin trail of small stars that looks like a wisp of smoke and then the two much bigger ones to the right of it? Well we need to aim for 'em and then keep 'em on the starboard side. I'm sure now we're that close I´ll be able to read the waters once the sun is up but," pointing due south "that's definitely where we need to head for."

Jake marked their position on the ship's map then charted a course due south; he had enough confidence in his friend to ask Martin to hoist sail and continue on their journey through the balmy moonlit night.

Once the sun was up India seemed to be able to steer instinctively toward their goal. He had been standing in the bow of the ship since daybreak concentrating hard, studying the waters when he suddenly cried out "Gawd almighty! Look, look, the sea children, they've come to meet us."

Jake headed for the bow wondering what all the commotion was about and saw his friend jumping up and down, waving and pointing and calling out to anyone within hearing. Following India's directions he looked over the side and saw a group of huge fish speeding alongside the ship, leaping out of the water as though spring loaded and he could just make out India screeching something about children.

His friend's excitement was infectious and remembering India's tale of the creatures that had pushed him ashore he laughed out loud. We've made it lads, we've made it!"

Sure enough, as dusk was falling, they heard a cry

from the crow's nest, "Land - Ho." Hauling all sails bar the foresails to slow their speed they maintained their course, anchoring just off a small group of islands until sun up.

At Jake's request the whole crew were assembled on deck so that he could run over once again the reason for visiting the islands, and so that India could acquaint them with some of the local customs.

"You all know we have come in the hope of being able to harvest a pretty remarkable plant which has proven to be a wonderful medicine. Once, if, we get permission to lift some of these plants I am hoping that they can be transplanted and grown successfully, some in the sugar plantation we are going on to in Jamaica, and some once we get back to England. All I can say is that when used properly, this plant works miracles. I appreciate that many of you are sceptical about my claims, but there is no doubt that it saved my father's life and God willing, if we are successful, it will save many other poor souls. Now, over to India."

Most of the men were already acquainted with these customs as India had spent many hours amusing his shipmates with tales from his past and with life on the islands. Many were indeed sceptical about the benefits of some plant but as they were being well paid to ply their trade they were happy to humour their delusional friends.

India was trembling with emotion. He never truly thought he would return to this place and the thought of seeing Narntac and his family, the family that had once been his, filled him at once with wild elation, dread and overwhelming sadness. He felt the physical pain of losing Narnsee strike him once again and was so grateful to have Jake alongside him to share this journey.

"Jake's right. The people on these islands used their

medicine on me or I'd 'av been a gonna and that's for sure. They was real good to me and I lived here with 'em for years, but I need to tell yer a few things. For starters, they don't wear many clothes, and the wimmin don't have no tops on."

This gave rise to a few ribald jokes and laughter.

"It ain't funny! That's the way they are; they just don't need 'em and they don't see no wrong in it. They ain't got none of our bad habits either. They don't steal, don't know what lies are and they don't do no-one any wrong, so we gotta be the same - or else!"

Martin Coleman took up India's warning. "You heard what India said. These people are very different from us so while we are here we respect them and their customs, and be assured gentlemen, that anyone who steps out of line will be locked in the brig for the duration of the voyage - and I am not joking! That is all. Now let's get those dinghies into the water.

The order was given but before the first craft had hit the surface several canoes appeared from inside the island's protective reef making their way speedily to The Elizabeth.

Copyright <u>Trudie Le Beau</u>

**

I asked my friend "Has your son decided what he wants to be when he grows up?"
"He wants to be a dustman", he replied.
"That's an unusual ambition to have at such a young age"
"Not really, he thinks that dustmen only work on Tuesdays"

In The Class Room

The teacher was telling the kids about the birds and the bees and she explained that when a man and a woman meet and fall in love, nine months later the stork usually brings them a little baby from its nest.

Little Gemma at the back of the class put her hand up and asks the teacher, 'Are you sure about the stork, miss? I think you're getting your birds mixed up 'cos my big sister just got a little baby and she said it was from a shack at the beach.'

**

I got a job at a bakery because I kneaded dough.

Velcro - what a rip off!

Don't worry about old age; it doesn't last.

I'm reading a book about anti-gravity. I just can't put it down.

**This article is taken with his permission from
Leapy Lee's weekly column in the Euro News
And was published in September 2017**

<u>Are the kids of today ruined or not?</u>

LEAPY LEE SAYS IT – OTHERS THINK IT.

The unbelievable hype and media hysteria surrounding the A-level exams has now become utterly ridiculous.

Every television channel this year was completely saturated with students elevated to minor celebrity status merely for opening up an envelope bursting into tears, hugging each other and jumping up and down.

The mind boggles. Even though the authorities vehemently denied tests had been dumbed down, they admit the privileged, often ungrateful bunch, have had the new test results 'scored more generously.' Oh that's ok then.

Story Telling Five

Apparently with the revised method of marking the authorities didn't want to cause the students too much 'unnecessary stress.' You really couldn't make it up.

There are even websites advising parents on how to deal with the diddums who didn't do too well. Advice includes relaxing techniques, comprising medication and exercise. They are also told to give them 'time to grieve' and teach them rhythmic breathing.

Parents are also informed they should be on the lookout for the signs of stress, raging from sobbing through tests, ears turning red to losing eye lashes! And what is the result of all this almost beyond belief pandering of these 'future leaders?'

Gratitude.? Don't make me laugh. Many of these sensitive little flowers actually see themselves as victims of oppression. One young madam actually insisted that because she suffered from anxiety and depression she should have been afforded special treatment and even allowed extended deadlines, because she was a slow reader.

If you ever wondered where the leftwing PC brigades actually manifests, look no further. The National Union of Students recently wanted to ban clapping and cheering because it 'triggered anxiety.' The hard on activists of the University of East Anglia took offence at what they saw as 'cultural appropriation' because a local restaurant handed out sombreros. Sussex actually wanted to ban the use of 'he' and 'she' as pronouns, because it made assumptions about identity.   Another student body wanted to ban Jamaican stew and Tunisian rice because it created 'racist micro-aggressions.'

Wha'?

This leftie lot also requested warnings before being exposed to offensive books, such as The Great Gatsby (violence towards woman) and even the Merchant of Venice, for its anti-somatic portrayal of Shylock.

No wonder they all lean towards Corbyn and his policies of simpering, cynical appeasement. Mark my words, this diversity happy bunch, with their self-centred utterly misplaced priorities will one day, if they find time to look up from their mobile phones, find their women clad in burkas, living under the yolk of sharia law and witnessing beheadings on the campus.

Never mind Jamaican stew. Let them see what happens in that scenario, when they try and protest that every TV show should have a transgender performer. 'Er what television? Heaven help them all.

Keep the faith. Love Leapy

Leapylee2002@gmail.com

**

"Passion is energy. Feel the power that comes from focusing on what excites you."

Oprah Winfrey

Parking

Paddy was driving down the street in a sweat because he had an important meeting and couldn't find a parking place. Looking up to heaven he said, 'Lord take pity on me. If you find me a parking place I will go to Mass every Sunday for the rest of me life and give up me Irish Whiskey!'
 Miraculously, a parking place appeared.
Paddy looked up again and said, 'Never mind, I found one.'

**

_WD-40_
The multi use product

WD-40 what a strange name – it was created by three technicians at the San Diego Rocket Chemical Company who were attempting to develop a water displacement compound to protect missile parts in 1953.

They were successful with the fortieth formulation, thus WD-40. The Corvair Company bought it in bulk to protect their atlas missile parts.

Ken East, one of the original founders, says 'there is nothing in WD-40 that could hurt you...it is made from fish oil.

SIX LITTLE STORIES

One: Once all the villagers decided to pray for rain. On the day of prayer all the people gathered, but only one boy came with an umbrella.

That's *FAITH.*

Two: When you throw babies in the air, they laugh because they know you will catch them.

That's *TRUST.*

Three: Every night we go to bed without any assurance of being alive the next morning, but still we set the alarms to wake up.

That's *HOPE.*

Four: We plan big things for tomorrow in spite of zero knowledge of the future.

That's *CONFIDENCE.*

Five: We see the world suffering, but still we get married and have children.

That's *LOVE.*

Six: On an old man's shirt was written a sentence 'I am not 80 years old; I am sweet 16 with 64 years of experience.'

That's *ATTITUDE.*

Last Man

The funeral notice stopped Fred dead in his tracks -
So, Bill had succumbed to his third heart attack ...
The Big C had claimed John back in ninety one
Mike suffered a stroke - next day he was gone

He cast his mind back a half century and more
to The Cradley Heath Kids - the incredible four
So fearless all, rambling and scrambling at will
through woods, heavy undergrowth, steepest of hills

So often regarded as the weakest of links,
the last man left standing now needed a drink
This sniveling lad often left holding coats
had become adept writing obituary notes.
Copyright Richard Seal 2017

**

WARNING -- When buying on Line.
Check out the seller carefully.
A friend spent $50 on a penis enlarger.

The swines sent him a magnifying glass.

The Instructions said, "Do not use in
direct sunlight"

Felix Wild
Continued from Story Telling Four

The following is the opening chapter of 'Felix Wild' (ISBN 978-1-911105-21-3) a historic novel written by Peter Broadbent to be published in Hardback in June 2017 by Chaplin Books (http://www.chaplinbooks.co.uk) 5 Carlton Way, Gosport, Hampshire PO12 1LN Tel +44(0)23 9252 9020. Contact Amanda Field. © Peter Broadbent

A brilliant piece of writing...the setting is a Court Room in the Seventeen Hundreds.

Chapter 1 PETTY SESSIONS

'Felix?'

'Yes, sir.'

'The minor misdemeanour was?'

'Not noted, sir.'

'I need a family name for the boy. Your family name, sir?' the Justice asks the Junior Clerk.

'Wildgoose sir,' replies the Clerk.

'No good. Can't inflict such a ridiculous birdlike name on the lad.'

'It is a well-respected and fashionable name of which I am the pr ...'

'That may be so, sir,' interrupts the Justice. He looks over at the public benches. 'Is there anyone in *the court willing to give a family name to the accused?'*

Silence.

Justice Braveheart looks directly at the Junior Clerk. 'Have you any objections to your family name being shortened, so that we can register it?'

'No objection, sir. I would be honoured, sir.' The Junior Clerk almost bends double, not knowing whether to remain seated or stand.

'Call the boy Wild. Log him as Felix Wild. Appropriate name for a feral foundling. Age?'

'Age unknown, sir,' says the Junior Clerk.

'Blast. Blast and damnation. We appear to have few, if any, details of the accused. Do we have a medical man in the court?'

Silence.

'Do we have a man with any medical qualification whatsoever in the place?'

At the back of the court a man wearing a grey coat, a chequered scarf draped over his shoulders and a wide-brimmed flax cap stands.

'I am a horse doctor, sir.'

'And your medical schooling sir?'

'I can assess the age of a horse by teeth and have done it accurately for thirty-one years, sir.'

'Could you determine the age of a young boy from his teeth?'

'In the absence of any other medical person, sir, I will attempt to.'

Story Telling Five

The Justice looks to the Senior Clerk who is bunched up in his corner. 'Is there any legal ruling against a horse doctor assessing the boy's age?'

The Senior Clerk hunches his shoulders.

'In heaven's name, man, stop your sulking. You do not have the brains to sulk effectively.'

The Senior Clerk wraps both his arms around his head.

The Justice waves his hand in the direction of the horse doctor.

'Present yourself to the front of the court. Examine the teeth of the accused and make an educated guess as to his age, in human not horse years. Remove your hat before entering my part of the court, sir.'

The court watches in silence as the horse doctor tosses his hat aside and shuffles to the front of the court. He holds the boy's mouth open while the smallest of the two Constables restrains the boy by holding his shoulders.

The boy stares at the ceiling.

'Well, man? What do his teeth tell you?'

The horse doctor stands up straight, unwinds a rogue section of his scarf and faces the Justice.

'It is difficult to ascertain accurate age. If he were a stallion I would improve his food mixture, however I ...'

'The boy is not and hopefully will never be a stallion, sir,' interrupts the Justice.

'Certainly he isn't, sir.'

'Age?'

'Between thirteen and fifteen, sir.'

Story Telling Five

'Return to your seat. Your name, sir?'

'Saddler, sir. James Saddler.'

'Note him down, Clerk,' says the Justice, watching the horse doctor slope back to his bench. Clearly in a rush to start his first case he taps his desk papers with his stone skull. 'Accused, you are to be known in this court and henceforth as Felix Wild aged fourteen. Do you understand?'

'Yes, sir,' says the boy.

'Charge details if you please, Clerk.'

The Junior Clerk gets to his feet and unrolls a parchment.

'Did on Tuesday the 20th day of August in the year of our Lord eighteen hundred and sixty, illegally attempt to steal a pocket timepiece, estimated value twelve shillings, from a Mister Samuel Longmire as he alighted from the harbour ferry at Gosport ramp, sir.'

'Witnesses?'

The Junior Clerk continues. 'The only plausible witness was a gentleman named Ernest Large, who has since left for foreign parts onboard HMS Vigilant in the service of Her Majesty, sir.'

'So he is of no blasted use to us here today,' states Justice Braveheart without looking up from his papers.

The Senior Clerk jumps to his feet, replaces his headgear and inhales deeply.

'With your permission, sir, I would point out that the accused was placed in Forton Gaol to await trial over two months since, sir. As a boy it is against ...'

'Do not attempt to spout your limited knowledge of the law to me, sir,' interrupts the Justice.

'That was never my intent, sir.'

'You are a legally trained nincompoop, sir. Felix Wild, what do say in response to the charge? Did you attempt to steal a pocket timepiece from a gentleman at the Ferry ramp in Gosport during August last?'

'No, sir,' says the boy.

'That is a definite defence, lad,' says Justice Braveheart, plucking another stray hair from his headgear. Turning to the Junior Clerk he asks, 'Was the timepiece actually removed from this man Longmire?'

'No, sir.'

'So how do we know the boy intended to take the timepiece?'

'By virtue of his proximity and behaviour, sir,' says the Senior Clerk replacing his headgear.

Justice Braveheart swerves to face the Senior Clerk. 'His proximity and his behaviour?'

'He had a hand almost on the hip of the gentleman, sir.'

'Almost ... blasted almost?'

'In the process of snatching the timepiece.'

'Do we have clear and indisputable evidence that the boy was intent on taking the timepiece?'

'Evidence of an experienced Constable standing in the vicinity, sir.'

'An experienced Constable?'

'Yes sir,' replies the Senior Clerk a little hesitantly. 'The accused is a vagrant child, sir, of no fixed abode and no parentage.'

'Which doesn't necessarily make him a thief.'

'Does it not, sir?'

'No, my good man, it does not.'

'If you say so, sir.'

'Is the aforementioned experienced Constable in the room?'

'Unfortunately not, sir.' says the Senior Clerk. 'He is presently in Forton gaol awaiting a trial date for a grave transgression.'

Justice Braveheart removes his headgear, slaps it on his elbow and replaces it on his head. 'I am dismissing this case.' He waves an angry arm at the courtyard door. 'I have the detritus of local humanity outside in the yard, all of whom thoroughly deserve my considered punishment. This young boy has done nothing wrong to my mind. The cost to the town of keeping a young boy behind bars is excessive. Case dismissed, Clerk. Dismissed.'

'As you say, sir,' replies the Senior Clerk.

'The case should never have been presented.'

'As you say, sir.'

'Any further information on Master Wild?'

Silence.

The Senior Clerk raises his hand. 'I beg your pardon, sir - what age shall I place alongside the boy's name, sir?'

'Fourteen. Have you not been paying attention to the case, sir?'

'I have, sir. Hanging on your every word, sir.'

'You are a stranger to the truth, my good man - a blasted stranger. Some time ago I clearly declared his age to be fourteen.'

Story Telling Five

The Senior Clerk nods. 'Fourteen years, sir. Thank you.'

'You are dismissed without charge, Felix Wild. I don't expect that you have any complaint about that?' says the Justice.

The larger of the two Constables elbows the boy in the ribs.

'The Justice is addressing you, boy,' he whispers. 'Say "no complaint sir" and "thank you".'

The boy looks directly at Justice Braveheart. 'No complaint, sir and thank you.'

The caped gentleman on the front row stands and salutes the court with his raised stick. 'Excuse me, Justice Braveheart, may I be permitted to speak to the court?'

'By all means. Please state your reason for interrupting proceedings, along with your name and occupation, sir.' Justice Braveheart settles himself in his chair and extracts a long-stemmed pipe from the folds of his coat.

The gentleman tips his stick to his forehead.

'Thank you, sir. My name is William Kettle. I am a gentleman of private means representing a large marine merchant in Portsmouth City. This week I am conducting business in the Royal Dockyard whilst residing at the Keppel's Head Hotel in Portsmouth - I have a friendship with the proprietor, Elizabeth Harrison. My permanent family residence is in London.'

'Please explain to the Court why a gentleman from our capital city should be accorded the privilege of

addressing this court, sir,' asks the Senior Clerk, keeping a weather-eye on Justice Braveheart.

'Sit yourself down, sir,' Justice Braveheart says to the Senior Clerk. 'Mister Kettle was addressing me directly. We are about to embark on an adult and gentlemanly conversation.'

The Senior Clerk nods apologetically and sits himself on the edge of a seat in his shadowed corner. He removes his headgear and stares at the floor between his feet.

'Continue Mister ...' says the Justice, removing his pipe.

'Kettle, sir - William Kettle,' says the standing gentleman. 'Thank you, sir. I am aware that the people of Gosport and Portsmouth have entrenched Naval connections. As such, they will understand the serious implications of the recent launch of the French vessel Gloire, the first ocean-going iron-clad warship. This vessel and her two sister vessels could upset the balance of naval power and have already initiated a seaborne invasion scare in Westminster, London. The situation was perceived to be so serious that Her Majesty herself asked the Admiralty if the Royal Navy was adequately equipped to counter any French iron-clad offensive. Parliamentary approval for the construction of a steel-hulled vessel was given and it is currently under construction in East London, sir.'

There are a number of shaking heads within the audience.

Story Telling Five

Justice Braveheart struggles to his feet, places his smoking pipe on the corner of his desk and looks directly at Mister Kettle.

'That, sir, was an excellent discourse on the current mistrust between the French and ourselves ... which is nothing new. I need to know in brief, sir, the reason for your interruption as we have little time to deal with the number of cases this morning.'

'I am looking to find an apprentice to further my business, having recently had the good fortune to earn myself a lucrative government contract ...'

'What contract, sir?'

'I am not permitted to divulge contract details, sir.'

'Understood. Continue.'

'I am informed that during his recent confinement the young boy, now named Felix Wild aged fourteen years, displayed an unusual artistic ability.'

'Did he?' splutters the Justice. 'What is this ability? Will someone tell me why I was not fully informed of the boy's ability?'

The Junior Clerk shrugs.

'I have a requirement for a marine artist, sir,' says Mister Kettle. 'A position that I have found difficult to fill despite much searching both here and in London. I would like to determine the young boy's ability should he be released into my care and without charge from this Session, sir.'

'More detail, sir,' says the Justice, preoccupied with a blemish on his coat collar. 'How did you learn of this boy's alleged artistic talent?'

Story Telling Five

'Over dinner last evening at my hotel I was informed that a young vagrant boy, with unusual artistic ability, was to be present at today's Session and would likely be released without charge. I am interested in all manner of artistic aptitude as I can use such persons within my business ...'

'How did you hear that the boy would be released without charge, sir?' interrupts the Justice, pointing his smoking pipe at the gentleman.

'Likely to be released without charge, sir,' replies Mister Kettle.

'How so?'

'My informant is a confidant of the legal service, sir.'

'A confidant of the legal service, sir?' Justice Braveheart slams the top of his desk. The paper pile shudders. 'What the hell does that mean? Give me details. Name of the confidant, sir.'

'I cannot, sir.'

'You will, sir,' says the Justice fondling his stick. 'Or I will exercise some of my judicial powers.'

'It was your brother-in-law Mister George Crofton, sir, who viewed the list of today's Session and your considered punishments.'

Justice Braveheart's mouth opens and closes.

'My brother-in-law is a charlatan, sir.'

'I have no opinion one way or the other, sir. But if you will confirm that the case against the boy is to be dismissed and that the boy can be released into my charge ...'

Justice Braveheart turns to his Senior Clerk.

'Can we legally agree to such a request?'

The Senior Clerk sulks silently.

Justice Braveheart turns to his Junior Clerk.

'Can we legally agree to such a request?'

'It would simplify and hasten proceedings, sir.'

'Boy!' Justice Braveheart glares at the accused. 'Look at me, boy!'

The large Constable jabs Felix in the ribs and nods towards the Justice.

Justice Braveheart waits until the boy raises his head.

'Boy, I have a mind to dismiss any charge against you as I have no credible witness to confirm your guilt. Normally I would return you to safe custody until deciding what is to be done with you. In the light of recent discussions with a gentleman in this court I propose to release you into the custody of a Mister .... err ...' He looks inquiringly at his Junior Clerk.

'Mister William Kettle, a gentleman of private means, presently residing at The Keppel's Head Hotel on the Hard at Portsmouth, sir.'

'I propose to release you into the custody of Mister William Kettle, a gentleman of private means, presently residing at The Keppel's Head Hotel in Portsmouth. Do you have any objection?'

Silence.

The smaller Constable whispers, 'Say "no sir".'

'No, sir.'

'Case dismissed then. Let the boy be released to the custody of Mister whatever-his-name-is, when all the papers are correctly raised. Clerk - make the

necessary notations. And get a written undertaking from the gentleman himself. Who is next?'

'The man Toby registered as Smith, sir,' says the Junior Clerk.

A stiff-backed Constable appears at the door.

'By your leave, sir. The accused known as Toby is unconscious and we are not able to revive him.'

'Is he alive and breathing?' asks the Justice, realigning his papers.

'I believe so, sir.

'Take him from the list. Revive him if you can. If not, we can organise for the rogue to be buried or otherwise disposed of.'

'Can you see Mistress Primula Waldrip then, sir ... out of list order?'

'Is she clean?'

'No, sir. She has recently pissed on her skirts.'

'Does she stink?'

'Yes, sir.'

'Dunk her in the creek. I will see her when both she and her skirts are clean and dry.'

'Dunk her in the creek, sir?'

'Yes. Damned woman. She is never clean. She lives caked in midden-muck and surrounded with foul, bodily gases. She is not, under any circumstances, to be allowed into this courtroom until she is declared clean. The place smells putrid as it is.'

'Aye aye, sir,' says the Constable in the doorway.

Justice Braveheart rises to his feet.

'Senior Clerk - I suggest you return to the place from whence you came unless you can contribute

anything to our proceedings.' He removes his headgear and hands it to his Junior Clerk. 'I hereby authorise a break of thirty minutes for refreshment. Public persons to remain in place. Thirty minutes, Junior Clerk. Do you have a timepiece?'

'Yes, sir.'

'Lend it to me so that I can judge the time. I can be found in the upstairs room of the George and Dragon in a dire emergency.'

'Court rise.'

Justice Braveheart scans the public seats.

'And if you superfluous malcontents think you can skip away for a quick libation, you can think again. Stay seated exactly where you are.' He skips out through a side door.

The flanking Constables escort the newly named Felix Wild out into the courtyard and hand him over to the coachman who is instructed to take him back to the gaol at Forton to collect his few belongings and to await his discharge papers.

Having signed the required papers, Mister William Kettle leaves the room twenty minutes after the Justice.

Primula Waldrip is escorted to Haslar Creek and unceremoniously thrown into its filthy waters. She wallows in the shallows, her grimy swathes flowing around her palpitating body. The Constables drag her out before she settles. She sprawls on the grass.

'Fancy a good long piss now,' she declares.

Toby opens one eye and decides to remain unconscious.

Copyright Peter Broadbent

We are sure this is right anyway who would want to make it up???

What is meant by the modern term referred to as

"POLITICAL CORRECTNESS"
The definition is found in 4 telegrams at the Truman Library and Museum in Independence, Missouri.

The following are copies of four telegrams between President Harry Truman and General Douglas MacArthur on the day before the actual signing of the WWII Surrender Agreement in September 1945.

The contents of those four telegrams below are exactly as received at the end of the war - not a word has been added or deleted!

(1) *Tokyo, Japan   0800-September 1,1945*

To: President Harry S Truman

From: General D A MacArthur

Tomorrow we meet with those yellow-bellied bastards and sign the Surrender Documents, any last minute instructions?

(2) *Washington, D C   1300-September 1, 1945*

To: D A MacArthur From: H S Truman

Congratulations, job well done, but you must tone down your obvious dislike of the Japanese when discussing the terms of the surrender with the press, because some of your remarks are fundamentally not politically correct!

(3) *Tokyo, Japan 1630-September 1, 1945*

To: H S Truman
From: D A MacArthur and C H Nimitz

Wilco Sir, but both Chester and I are somewhat confused, exactly what does the term politically correct mean?

(4) *Washington, D C 2120-September 1, 1945*

To: D A MacArthur/C H Nimitz

From: H S Truman

Political Correctness is a doctrine, recently fostered by a delusional, illogical minority and promoted by a sick mainstream media, which holds forth the proposition that it is entirely possible to pick up a piece of shit by the clean end!

Now, with special thanks to the Truman Museum and Harry himself, you and I finally have a full understanding of what 'POLITICAL CORRECTNESS' really means…..

Santa's Been

Sally frowned down at her massive turkey, wrestling with the annual defrosting dilemmas. Feeling faint and exhausted for the third consecutive day, she wondered where on Earth Frank has got to with the sherry and mince pies. She decided that Santa would have to make do with wine and cheese next year.

In the next room her children were tussling around the tree, sneaking chocolate decorations and hoping Santa would come early in the morning. They jostled and pointed as dusk's gloom was lifted by the arrival of snow. As large flakes settled steadily, a squirrel headed for his burrow, a fox retreated to her hole and sheltering birds watched the earth disappear with fear for their Christmas lunch.

Spending a bleary-eyed evening cruising around superstore aisles in low gear, left Frank feeling deeply uninspired. Familiar items were picked on autopilot, the shopping list unread. He stopped instead in one corner, where Christmas biscuits, Belgian, had lain neglected since the Summer. Sensing their plight, Frank ended their wait, not worried that the box was two weeks out of date. He forgot both the sherry and mince pies, but there was a great festive deal on the beer ...

Santa and his wife wake up at three o'clock with the alarm's jolt. Frank rubs his unshaven chin, trying to blink away Christmas Eve excesses. His revival is kick-started by a cigarette, while Sally struggles to drag herself out of bed, and cannot face anything more than half a cup of tea. They know they must fill the stockings before the kids appear wondering if he's been. Hearing stirring behind doors an hour or so later, Santa is glad to celebrate with a glass of the hair of the dog.

As a young girl, Sally was entranced by the magic of the Christmas tree - baubles, bright, frosted looking good enough to eat, angels hanging, chocolate bells running the risk of melting by fairy lights. Grown up, the tree now looks smaller, somehow limp, faded, tired .. Suddenly, briefly, she feels inspired by the sight of the fairy from her childhood; still here, just barely, so fragile and delicate, enshrined in pine.

Frank embraced his childhood Christmas morning joy with special stockings swelled by toys, games, chocolate, fruit and nuts ... He had been keen to pass the tradition down to his kids, but always heard mumble grumbles despite their Dad's delight, groaning at the sight of threadbare socks filled with tat. He finally faces the rueful realisation that Santa's socks fall flat.

In pride of place in the living room, pussy's pillow is a sight to behold – fur coated, poke prodded, much kneaded. The fabric is fray degraded, brittle with spittle, scent savoured with flavours, favours. Her new cushion, a be-ribboned Christmas gift - sniff inspected, spite-spiked is destined never to be touched.

Granddad used to be grainy in photos, black-and-white, lacking humour in his youth; moustachioed, restrained by a grey waistcoat and suit. As an old man, he looks happy, relaxed, clean-shaven; in scent of liquorice and pipe-smoke, he has turned cheerful in colour, chuckling in his Christmas cardigan.

Smiling wistfully, raising her tea cup, Granny watches presents being torn open by grandchildren. Her eyes drift across to her daughter's face, pale and drawn yet ablaze with joy, settling in her loving warmth. The scene shifts - the old lady now becomes Mum, who is a child again, lost for a moment in a frenzy of wrapping paper.

Having helped Santa, Sally manages to hang on a while longer to serve the Christmas dinner. She powers through the Turkey and beef ... Her death during the Queen's speech, the still form sitting in her chair defies grief. The pudding is still warm; leftovers not having been sorted or stored is such bad form.

Copyright Richard Seal 2017

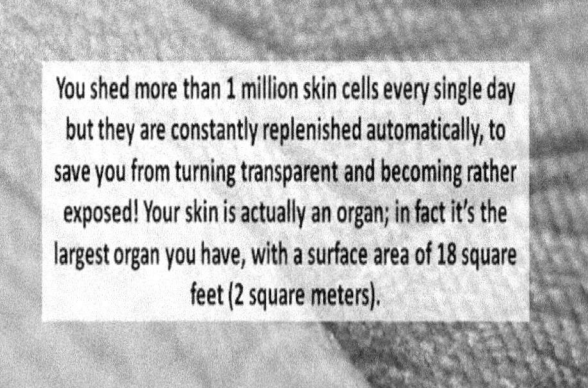

You shed more than 1 million skin cells every single day but they are constantly replenished automatically, to save you from turning transparent and becoming rather exposed! Your skin is actually an organ; in fact it's the largest organ you have, with a surface area of 18 square feet (2 square meters).

Bruce the Rooster

Sarah was in the fertilized egg business. She had several hundred young pullets and ten roosters to fertilize the eggs. She kept records and any rooster not performing went into the soup pot and was replaced.

This took a lot of time, so she bought some tiny bells and attached them to her roosters. Each bell had a different tone, so she could tell from a distance which rooster was performing. Now, she could sit on the porch and fill out an efficiency report by just listening to the bells.

Sarah's favourite rooster, old Bruce, was a very fine specimen but, this morning she noticed old Bruce's bell hadn't rung at all! When she went to investigate, she saw the other roosters were busy chasing pullets, bells-a-ringing, but the pullets hearing the roosters coming, would run for cover.

To Sarah's amazement, old Bruce had his bell in his beak, so it couldn't ring. He'd sneak up on a pullet, do his job, and walk on to the next one.

Sarah was so proud of old Bruce, she entered him in the Darwin Show and he became an overnight sensation among the judges.

The result was the judges not only awarded old Bruce the "No Bell Peace Prize" they also awarded him the "Pulletsurprise" as well. Clearly old Bruce was a politician in the making.

Who else but a politician could figure out how to win two of the most coveted awards on our planet by being the best at sneaking up on the unsuspecting populace and screwing them when they weren't paying attention?

Vote carefully in the next election. You can't always hear the bells.

**

A fine is a tax for doing wrong. A tax is a fine for doing well.
He who laughs last, thinks slowest.
Change is inevitable, except from a vending machine.
Nothing is foolproof to a sufficiently talented fool.

Cat Christmas

Wrapping paper, semi-shredded,
is strewn around the living room
with decorations, having fallen,
lying amongst broken baubles.
On Christmas morning the tree
has toppled casting little fairy
from top branch into fireplace.
Several presents are damaged
before family's day has begun,
but cats lick their paws, content
they have already had their fun.

Copyright Richard Seal 2017

**

The Making of Man and Woman

The first day, God created the dog and said: "Sit all day by the door of your house and bark at anyone who comes in or walks past. For this I will give you a life span of twenty years."

The dog said, "That's a long time to be barking. How about only ten years and I'll give you back the other ten?"
And God said that it was good.

On the second day, God created the monkey and said, "Entertain people, do tricks, and make them laugh. For this, I'll give you a twenty-year life span"

The monkey said, "Monkey tricks for twenty years? That's a pretty long time to perform. How about I give you back ten like the dog did?"
And God again said that it was good.

On the third day, God created the cow and said, "You must go into the field with the farmer all day long and suffer under the sun, have calves and give milk to support the farmer's family. For this, I will give you a life span of sixty years."
The cow said "That's kind of hard to want me to live for sixty years. How about twenty and I'll give back the other forty?"
And God agreed it was good.

On the fourth day, God created humans and said, "Eat, sleep, play, marry and enjoy your life. For this, I'll give you twenty years."
But the human said, "Only twenty years? Could you possibly give me my twenty, the forty the cow gave back, the ten the monkey gave back, and the ten the dog gave back; that makes eighty, okay?"
"Okay," said God, "You asked for it."

So that is why for our first twenty years, we eat, sleep, play and enjoy ourselves. For the next forty years, we slave in the sun to support our family. For the next ten years, we do monkey tricks to entertain the grandchildren. And for the last ten years, we sit on the front porch and bark at everyone.

Life has now been explained to you.

**

ATTORNEY: This *myasthenia gravis*, does it affect your memory at all?

    WITNESS: Yes.

ATTORNEY: And in what ways does it affect your memory?

    WITNESS: I forget.

ATTORNEY: You forget? Can you give us an example of something you forgot?

**

ATTORNEY: The youngest son, the 20 year-old, how old is he?

    WITNESS: He's 20 - much like your IQ.

Percy accepts that we are all different however he was once totally deaf in his right ear and here explains how it was cured.

Deafness?

It was some time ago, before we moved to Spain, when I was interested in an article by a learned Doctor who was arguing that some illnesses are in the mind, and the only reason we cannot cure them ourselves is because of our teaching as youngsters. His point was the human body cures itself in many ways and quoted by saying 'if you lose a finger nail a new one will grow or if you cut yourself then the body will repair the damage.'

He also went on to explain and quote cases where people have got over poor health by the sheer trust that they could. He also stated he could see no reason if someone lost a finger then with the sincere belief that you can, it should be possible to grow a new one.

All that is very controversial, however I do consider it is possible to get over some ill health if previous teaching are put aside and total trust in one's own internal immune system. Please do not get me wrong I am not advocating the dismantling of the Health Service as there are many types of poor health that need the expertise of the medical profession.

Story Telling Five

Over a period of time I had seen many specialists for hearing loss, most seem to be in the business of selling aids at lofty prices. I was also referred by a doctor to the Hearing Clinic at the hospital. After sitting in a box and listening to various pinging sounds pumped through ear phones, the consultant pronounced I was deaf in my right ear. There was nothing he could do and advised me to buy a hearing aid and then made it clear by saying, 'You only need one...don't let them sell you two!'

About six years ago an article from an Ear Specialist appeared in the 'Round Town News.' A popular paper published in Spain for the English community. I say an article but in real terms it was an advertisement. The Ear Consultant was stating that there was no need for people to have loss of hearing as the ear is quite capable of healing itself. He went on to explain that is why our ears on the side of our heads grow larger as we get older.

The expert was offering those with hearing loss to visit him and he, with the help of specialist ear drops could make an improvement without the need for hearing aids. At the time I was wearing an aid in my right ear so the article was of interest. On the other hand as we were due to leave for England I thought I would wait for our return before following it up.

However, whilst in the UK we went shopping in Tesco who at the time were doing a promotion on ear drops. The coincidence of the article in Spain and the information in the store was not easy to ignore, so I bought them. The instructions said they would remove tightly packed ear wax which had built up over the years and they were to be used three times a day which I followed.

There was no immediate result, nevertheless, I persevered. It was about eighteen months later I awoke one morning to the sound of birds singing. Not unusual until I realised I was laying on my good ear and I shouldn't be able to hear anything. Then I realised it was my right deaf one, which was hearing the beautiful sound. The pillow was a yellow colour where the ear drops had removed the old wax.

Today, although I still use different types of ear drops, pure olive oil, about once every three days, I can hear very well including stereo, and the hearing aid was discarded a long time ago. Although, like most people, I find it difficult hearing in noisy situations, nevertheless it would be nice to think this article has been of some help to similar sufferers.

Copyright Percy Chattey 2017

**

ATTORNEY: How was your first marriage terminated?

WITNESS: By death.

ATTORNEY: And by whose death was it terminated?

WITNESS: Take a guess.

**

ATTORNEY: ALL your responses MUST

be oral, OK? What school did you go to?
WITNESS: Oral...

Never Forget

James often had a little smile to himself, bemused about the fact that he had lived such a long life. He seemed to have escaped unscathed from the effects of smoking cigarettes throughout most of his adult life; he had always enjoyed drinking, and had never been a big fan of eating healthily either. His idea of exercise had seldom extended far beyond a half-hearted jog to the pub when last orders was getting a bit too close for comfort ...

Sensing the anticipation starting to build around him, James glanced at his watch and was not surprised to see that the old year now had only a few minutes remaining. He drained his pint with relish and finished his last sausage roll. While the family and friends gathered around were all younger than him, he always felt happy and comfortable in their company. He was enveloped by a familiar beery warmth as he was helped to his feet.

As he linked arms with his lovely nieces, James wondered how many times he had heard 'Auld Lang Syne' on New Year's Eve. It seemed to have a deeper resonance since his beloved wife Ellen had passed, of course .. Stepping forward he could sense her beside him, her thigh pressed against his as always, her rich voice singing with passion deep within, while his mother's hand continued to squeeze joy from his heart as the chorus reached a crescendo.

As the ring broke, James felt his Dad's arms holding him safely, keeping him steady on his first bike ... The song continued to echo throughout his being, heightening his senses as the New Year chimes heralded hugs and kisses from loved ones in the old man's past and present. Through the laughter and tears, old acquaintances never to be forgotten.
Copyright Richard Seal 2017

 *A VERY HAPPY NEW YEAR TO ALL OUR READERS, MAY THE SUN SHINE DOWN ON YOU AND THE BANK MANAGER GREETS YOU WITH PRIDE!!!*

THERE ARE FIVE PREVIOUS ISSUES OF STORY TELLING AND ANOTHER WILL BE OUT AGAIN SOON

www.percychatteybooks.com